Bipolar is Not My Family's Secret

Unveiling - Taking off the Mask

Itchy Mae

authorHOUSE®

AuthorHouse™
1663 Liberty Drive
Bloomington, IN 47403
www.authorhouse.com
Phone: 833-262-8899

Published by AuthorHouse 05/22/2024

ISBN: 979-8-8230-2664-2 (sc)
ISBN: 979-8-8230-2665-9 (e)

Library of Congress Control Number: 2024909847

Print information available on the last page.

This book is dedicated to Reverend Caleb Benjamin Gardner in Loving memory of his transition to Heaven on April 14, 2016.

CONTENTS

FOREWORD

I AM FELECIA MCDANIEL, a fellow traveler on the winding road of life. As we embark on this journey together, I want you to know that even though I have a degree in Special Education for the Emotionally Impaired; I speak not from the pedestal of scholarly credentials, but from the depths of lived experiences. Mental health has woven its threads intricately through the fabric of my existence, shaping my role as a mother, grandmother, and a caregiver.

My journey has led me through the corridors of schools, where I've dedicated years to nurturing and supporting children with diverse needs. At home, I've stood alongside my daughters, navigating the challenges and joys of parenthood, as they care for their own children, each with their unique journey.

I've known, Joi Spencer for eight years. Joi, whose name describes her well, is my sorority sister. We became acquainted when she approached me and inquired about a committee which I served on. Joi was a perfect fit. We both are mothers, grandmothers, and Christians. As the author of this book, she is well qualified to speak on mental illness due to her real-life experiences and she is transparent with readers on how mental illness affects a family.

Joi offers not just insights, but empathy - a shared understanding born of shared struggles. Together, let us explore the nuances of the human experience and celebrate the resilience of the human spirit. In conclusion, I have reviewed the book and I highly recommend it to other readers.

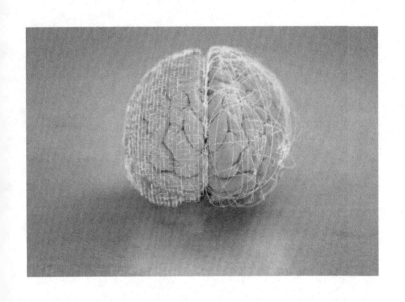

INTRODUCTION

THE *FIRST* SEQUEL exposed Itchy Mae's family life, bullying, dealing with molestation, and how her father had bipolar disorder with Schizophrenic tendencies; furthermore, it took twelve years to come back with sequel two. The *second* sequel is also written in third person and will cover the life of Itchy being a teenager attending high school in an urban neighborhood, college life, dating, marriage and exposing the enemy. In this sequel, I gratefully acknowledge my daughter for her invaluable collaboration, unwavering support, and creative input that have enriched every page with her unique prospective as a co-author writing Her story and poetry exposing the enemy from her prospective.

The way the writer in me evolved is not by reinventing myself it was more about re-imagining life despite the card's life dealt me and circumstances realized. It expounds on having a foundation of determination, and Christian morals and building a personal relationship with God. This book aims to encourage people suffering from depression, suicidal thoughts, and anxiety that there is hope. After you come out of denial and realize you are not the only person dealing with a chemical imbalance, seek professional help through therapy. The enemy known as bipolar disorder must be exposed to educate more families on how to deal with it once it rears its ugly face that changes your emotional and mental behavior.

It is not wise to keep this a secret or bottled up inside. In past years it was a stigma in the black community to publicly admit you see a therapist or psychiatrist. You cannot figure this out alone. It was known as taboo for people of color to seek counseling and therapy.

Most black families pass down the tradition of praying to the Lord and keeping your business (family secret) to yourself. In my experience, you must first pray for God's guidance, ask God to keep your mind and actively seek medical advice for a diagnosis. When a diagnosis is identified, you may require medication, therapy, and tips to sustain long-term maintenance care. The whole idea surrounding the series of short stories is being transparent to my readers that life happens; some things are within our control while other factors are not. All I have ever attempted to do is exemplify a positive attitude about life with a SMILE and live life on purpose serving Jehovah God, Jesus Christ, and relying on the Holy Spirit to help guide me and not just exist during my time on planet earth. My purpose is serving my community and helping others.

ACKNOWLEDGEMENTS

ALL GRATITUDE AND thanks goes to Claudia L. Scroggins, Reverend Caleb B. Gardner deceased 4/2016, Makayla Lynne' Spencer, Felecia McDaniel, Dr. Jacquelyn G. Wilson, Ramonda Hollenquest & Tracey L. Wicks, M.A., LPC, and everyone who inspired me to continue the sequels. Thank you to my mother, Claudia L. Scroggins, for giving me hope to 'KEEP LIVING.' Also, in loving memory of my father (Rev Caleb B. Gardner) for giving me an 'APPRECIATION OF LIFE' to tell my story.

My Father always instilled in his daughters being a virtuous woman that is described in the Bible, Proverbs 31:10-13.

To my darling daughter Makayla Lynne' Spencer, who awakened my soul from a dark place and allowed me to become transparent, speak boldly, and persistent in pushing through to achieve the best while gaining self-love and light to encourage her to "shine bright like a diamond." Being her mother has been a blessing and never a burden. We are no longer in denial.

CHAPTER ONE

Life In High School

THE YEAR IS **1980** September and for Itchy Mae it is the time to attend a new school. Her mom yells, "Itchy Mae hurry up, we are about to leave in a minute." She begged her mom to allow her to catch the bus. "Please, I'm old enough!" Her mom says, "No", we will take you to school; there is no way you will ride the Grand River bus by yourself. Itchy stumps down the stairs and mumbles under her breath. "Will she ever let me grow up?" Itchy went outside and jumped in the back seat of the car; my stepfather, whom we called (Poppa) was retired from General Motors; he would drive my mom to work daily. Itchy's mom worked for *City National Bank*

in the Penobscot Building, located in Downtown Detroit on Griswold.

As they turned off our street and drove down Grand River, Itchy was excited and couldn't wait. She did not want to go to the neighborhood school Mackenzie because she refused to fight for another four years. On the way to school, there were four other high schools in a closer vicinity, Mackenzie, Cody, Central & Northwestern, to get to Murray Wright High School.

They were approaching West Warren; as Itchy looked out the window, she could see the Post Office on Grand River, and then she saw the school's tennis court and the one-level brick building. Itchy couldn't wait to get inside. Poppa pulled over at the light, and I kissed my mom and took off running across Grand River through the Tennis Court across the field, never looking back, and Itchy could hear her mom fussing girl slow down. Itchy ran through the side door, and the security guard, McGee, directed me to the gym to register for classes. All Itchy could think was she is in high school now, with a brand-new start. Itchy had a plan, and it did not include fighting; this was a fresh start.

While standing in line to register for classes, she could feel someone looking at her, and so she looked up to see this cute boy with curly jet-black hair dressed very neatly that caught her eye. Itchy act as though she didn't notice him because she figure he was looking at someone else he knew. Itchy focused on registering for classes thinking she didn't know anyone else; however, four other students from *Charles R. Drew Middle School* were also in line:

Athena, Ursula E., Robin, and John (Terrence). Itchy attended *Philip Murray Wright* because it was a Trade School and offered courses like Cosmetology, Nursing, Auto Mechanics, and Culinary Arts. Itchy was there to become a Cosmetologist and open her salon one day. The principal was Mr. Robert Boyce, and Assistant Principal was Mrs. Woodhouse. Itchy Mae counselor was the most extraordinary, Mrs. Tatum. The school's mascot was Snoopy, he was the Pilot, and the school colors were blue and gold.

In Itchy's first year of High School, the first two girls she met were cousins named Tracey & Lisa. Itchy fit in just fine and became little Ms. Popular, she tried out for the track team and made it. She also joined the Booster Club. As for the cheer team, she didn't make the team due to having beat deafness which is refer to as rhythm impaired.

Itchy parents gave her a ride to school daily, and sometimes they were running late, so Itchy received a note from the attendance office that her mother would have to bring Itchy in and sign a form for them to get excused because of being tardy added up to absences. While waiting in the attendance office, guess who walks past? Mr. Douglas. He looks over at Itchy and says, "it is sure good to see you." Her mom has a puzzled look on her face. Then he brings his big bald head into the attendance room and asks Itchy, "have you been sick or something," Her mother replies NO; why do you ask? Oh, I haven't seen her in my English class in months. Itchy's mom turns to her and snatches her up, saying, "WHAT is he talking

ITCHY MAE

about." There is silence in the room, and you could hear crickets. Itchy knew then that her life was over. She was nervous the whole day and scared to go home.

When Itchy arrived home, it appears that her mom has called two of her sister's homes to talk to her? Itchy is the youngest and the only one still living at home. One of her sisters was away at College, Oakland University, and her other sister lived about five miles away. Itchy's mom explained to the pair what she did, and the look they gave her was not reassuring.

Itchy mom told her to, "go upstairs" the next thing she knew her mom pulled the belt out and start whooping her butt. They couldn't get a word in. Itchy tried to run up the stairs, and her mom would pull her back down the stairs. There is an entire mirrored wall when you walked in the front door to the left of the stairs. While lying on the floor trying to catch her breath, Itchy looked into the mirror and knew the meaning of an absolute beat down. After returning to school the next day, her mom prepared a document that each of her teachers had to sign every day to prove she attended their class. Itchy had to participate in summer school for English and Algebra and aced them both. The lesson is not to skip class to play games you are in school to learn and prepare yourself for college, so in your adult life, you develop good work and learning habits that will help you succeed. Two of the classes cut were English class, Mr. Douglas, and Typing Ms. Stewart taught, and she was a class act, no-nonsense teacher. Itchy was tired of getting her knuckles popped with the ruler by

Ms. Stewart for looking at the keyboard, so she decided she would skip.

As far as Mr. Douglas's class Itchy enjoyed his class and his teaching style; however, it was a popular Lunch period, third hour, and she didn't want to miss out on playing Tunk or Back Gammon/Acey-deucey. After this is when *sugar honey iced tea* goes downhill.

The year is **1981**, and Itchy is a sophomore in high school attending *Murray Wright High School*. She went by 'Private Joi' which was on the back of her Cosmetology varsity jacket. **Ronald Reagan** became President, and the United States experienced Reaganomics; this is a term referred to by many people living in urban cities. Before Ronald Reagan ran for office, he was an actor in Hollywood.

During his two terms in office, he continued his acting career in the White House by pretending he cared about middle or lower-class people. He cared so much that he changed family kitchens drastically with a thick block of cheese that made the best macaroni and cheese grilled cheese sandwiches.

Many referred to this wax paper-covered delicatessen as government cheese. Everyone knew someone that could get them some of this cheese; regardless of if, they were on public assistance or a senior citizen that received government cheese, and they would kindly share it. Focus Hope and other organizations had food programs for the less fortunate would distribute the cheese regularly.

The year Earth Wind & Fire released, **"Let's Groove."** Itchy Mae sister graduated from Oakland University and moved to Houston, Texas. Itchy would miss her, but she would never let her know that! Her sister had a going away party and invited all her Sorority sisters. Itchy and her cousin Kim were the DJs. Believe it or not, they had that basement rocking.

When they put this one record on the turntable and the needle hit the record, they all went crazy and danced in a line following one another while making this weird squeaking sound and holding their pinky finger up. The song was Prince's Controversy album burning up the turntables. Itchy's sister yells, turn it down before mom hears that and makes us turn it off. She quickly turned it down because she didn't want to get in trouble with their mom, nor did she want her sister to make them leave the party. A couple of days later she moves to Houston, Texas.

In **1982** Itchy was baptized at the family church, Holy Cross Missionary Baptist Church, and my dad, an Evangelist, gave me a White King's James Bible with a poem he had written called "Appreciation of Life." By this time, Itchy was more active in church and song in the youth choir, and on many Thursdays, she would walk from school after track practice to choir rehearsal. The family church was right down the street from Northwestern High School, so she would walk west down Grand River, and when she got to the *Olympia Stadium*, where the Red Wings first played Hockey, she turn to the right and cut through Northwestern softball field. This is also the year Itchy, and her friends turn sixteen and celebrate by having sweet sixteen parties. Not for Itchy, though; her mother was so strict she wasn't having a party or even allowed the privilege of being a hostess or attending her friend's sweet sixteen parties, and Itchy was mad about it!

Itchy had formed a friendship so tight with Tracey & Lisa, and they both were on the cheer team. Lisa also ran on the track team with her. Itchy also met the cute boy on the track team that moved from New Jersey, that wore the most incredible brush waves. He was an honor student, and made her laugh nonstop. He kept her laughing and giggling so much that she was fascinated and charmed by him and lost her virginity to him. This occurred on a half day of school at his parent's house and the regret was strong. She was baptized earlier that year and had broken her vow to God to remain abstinent until marriage. She learned early to watch out for distractions to keep you from pleasing God. Itchy other groups of friends were her cosmetology girls: Robyn, Ursula T, Pearl, Glenna, Amanda, Carolyn, Algina, Noreen, Yvette, Denise (Niecy) & Kim. The group of young ladies would walk from the *Wilbur Wright* building over to *Philip Murray*. Some of her favorite teachers in high school were Mrs. Mary Muckles, a cosmetology teacher. Mr. Bobby Carr was the biology teacher, and Ms. Bunton was the track coach who could do an awesome Chinese split and weighed over two hundred pounds. Never underestimate a person's size their flexibility will shock you.

High School was different from Middle School as far as fighting and gaining friends.

Northeastern closed, and a lot of its students transferred to *Murray Wright*. Out of the four years, Itchy had no fights, just one slapping match with Kelly from ROTC in their freshman year, and the same year, they became friends. Some of the students who attended Murray Wright came from two notable projects, *Jeffries* and the *Brewster's,* and students traveled from the East and West side of town; however, we were like one big blue and gold family. We also had the students from the number's streets and the north end. Don't get it wrong. There were fights between the projects and the football team. When it came down to other school rivalries, we stuck together. Many people still claim to this very day 'Pilot 4 Life'. Itchy became close friends with Ursula T. in her cosmetology class that lived in the Brewster Projects. Itchy Mae parents would drop her off and pick her up after hanging out at her house to get her hair done and prepare for hair shows. Ursula also came from a family of four girls.

APPRECIATION OF LIFE

Give me Life
To live for thee
Give me life
And set me free
Give me life
To do thy will
Give me life
With which love to fill
Give me life
This earth to trod
Give me life
To love my God
Give me life
To love my God
Give me life
With all my heart
Give me life
To speak, teach, and preach thou word
Give me life
To thou may be heard
Give me life
To hold your hand
Give me life
To walk your land
Give me life
To run this race
Give me life
To see thy face

Give me life
To praise thy name
Give me life
But not in vain
Give me life
To please thy cause
Give me life
To death pause

Author: Rev. Caleb B. Gardner

Time flies by when you are having fun, and the summer has ended, and Itchy's sister had a beautiful wedding in July, and now it is the fall of **1983** and Itchy's senior year. Itchy scheduled to take pictures at Foxx Photography Studio, and she made posters to campaign for class treasurer, which she won, and worked in the school bookstore collecting senior dues and selling supplies to students. This year, Itchy would wake up to WJLB FM radio station to Mason & Company in the mornings. Then at night, chill and listen to WGPR FM radio to Mojo. It was nothing for Mojo to have the battle of two artists and let the music play for three hours without interruptions, and everyone knew that he was either sleeping or flying high. Mojo was known for saying, "tie a knot at the end of the rope and hold on."

Itchy and her one friend that lived in Brewster projects would lose contact after high school and reconnect in 2000 while living on the east side of Detroit in an area called East English Village. Ursula T is now married with two children and doing well. It shows that when a young person is confident, focused, educated, and works hard, they do not have to become a product of their environment. Itchy started young as a romantic she had three love interests in high school. Her first was the visionary, cute guy that kept her laughing. Her boyfriend of two years, that played football with a great smile and bow-legged, which she dated him from sophomore to senior year. He was the only person she shared the story about the awful man fondling her. Itchy broke up with her boyfriend a few months before Prom, which was the silliest thing she could have ever done

11

and end up going to the Prom alone after being stood up. Lesson learned you reap what you sow and treat people the way you want to get treated.

Rewind, there was also the young man Itchy saw in the lunchroom her freshmen year registering for classes, which later broke her heart after high school and went to the Army.

It is May of **1984.** Itchy had found the sharpest evening gown while looking through the Ebony magazine and decided she wanted this dress made for her Prom in beautiful royal blue, which was her favorite color. Itchy's mother close friend, Mrs. Ethel's Halliburgh mother, did an extraordinary job making the dress.

The dress had layers that went around and down the entire dress like cake layers that was stunning! Itchy was standing in the living room when she got a call that her Prom date would not be going to the Prom. Mom shocked me when she asked, where does this boy live? Itchy called him back to get the address, and her parents did a non-violent drive-by. My mom and stepfather pulled up in a Yellow Buick Park Avenue with gangster white walls with spoke rims, and the young man came down to the car while his family stood on the porch, and he began to tell his lie. He said, "his uncle was supposed to get his tuxedo had too much to drink and forgot to pick it up, and he didn't have anything else to wear."

Keep in mind this was not his Prom; he was a junior and one of the school's top basketball players. My mom politely said, well, it would have been nice to know this earlier, and maybe it would have been something that we could have done. My side of the story is that he wanted to go to the Prom in a limousine or rental car.

It was tradition to get a rental car and, even better, if you came in a limousine back in the day. Itchy's class buddy Robyn and her boyfriend, that attended Central High School, came to Prom in a limo.

See, what had happened was Itchy had reserved a rental car from Metro Airport, and when it was time to pick up the car, all her plans fell through. The credit card holder had to have a driver's license. Itchy had the MasterCard, and my cousin Kim had the driver's license and was not going to be a driver of the rental car. Itchy called and told her date that they could take her mom's car, which was a brown Chevy Monza, and he paused and said, I'll call you back, and never did. He had a super-size of nerves talking about nerves, and it was a girl's Prom night.

Itchy would not let one monkey stop no show, so she had her parents drop her off at *Lansdown*e for dinner and had dinner with her class buddies sister, Darlene, and her date Greg, and then rode with them to the Prom, which was in Windsor Canada at Cleary Auditorium.

It was an incredible year for the Murray Wright Graduating Class of 1984. There was the historical moment the Tigers won the World Series, and the city celebrated big time. The graduation took place at *Ford Auditorium*. Graduation was bittersweet because Itchy's mother, three sisters, and Cousin Kim attended the ceremony. Her dad could not attend due to having a nervous breakdown the previous year and was admitted to Northville Regional Psychiatric Hospital, which was renamed in 1972 formerly Northville State Hospital.

After graduation realizing, Itchy formed friendships that resulted in staying in touch with two girls and one guy. My high school class buddy Robyn and we are still in contact until this very day. She lives in North Carolina with her husband, two daughters, and a son. They were married on Valentine's Day in 1998. Itchy was a hostess at her wedding and Robyn was a hostess at my wedding in 1991.

As for Itchy day one- best friend, Lisa from *Charles R Drew Middle School*, they never lost contact! This girl was determined to keep in touch. She stopped by Itchy's mothers house whenever she moved and gave her the new address and phone number. She had two children in high school and married the boy's father in December 1988. Then in 1994, she had another son and now lives in California. Her husband, Charles "Chuck," passed in July 2015 after 20 years of battling Sarcoidosis.

CHAPTER TWO

College and Meeting Celebrities

THE YEAR IS **1984,** and it is Itchy's first year of college. Her mother's desire for her four daughters to get an undergraduate college degree to achieve better opportunities in the corporate world. She was unable to attend college after graduating from Rosenwald High School in Kentucky, class of 1951. She moved from the south one year after high school and married moving north to Chicago Illinois.

Now Itchy was not too thrilled about going to college and wanted to work in a hair salon as a cosmetologist and own her Salon one day. When Itchy finished high school, she acquired 1500 credit hours toward cosmetology and just had to take her state board exams to become a licensed cosmetologist. During high school, she maintained over 3.0, and she was more substantial in math than in English.

She was not comfortable taking test and never enjoyed reading. Primarily reading was a more vital point posing comprehension problems, and somewhat embarrassed about it.

Her reading aloud skills were good; however, her comprehension was horrible. She had to take the reading proficiency test twice in high school. Once the student passes the test, the diploma's seal of completion, and you also receive a certificate. After the college academic advisor eliminating the cosmetology courses, in the end, the final GPA was 2.5.

Oakland University Summer Support Program was for students below 2.8. The late Mr. Hurst was the Director, and Mr. Robert Douglas was the Assistant Director; both men were positive male images. Two weeks after graduation, Itchy had to begin taking college courses. Then anxiety would kick in, and to no avail. Itchy would not test well at times, so there was fear of not being successful in college. There was no chance to say goodbye to her friends and go to the different graduation parties that we now call open houses. No longer working in Rose's Classic Style Room as a shampoo girl, the dream of owning a salon one day was quickly fading. Rose's Classic Style Room was in the Northwest Activity Center.

During that summer **of 1984**, Itchy Mae met the Piston players. Isaiah Thomas even autographed my high school yearbook after one of their practices held at Oakland University gym and the Lions practice on the football field. During the winter months, in their leisure time, Itchy and some friends would go to the cafeteria, which we called Saga, and get a food tray, bright orange or yellow and then go out to the back of the campus by the tennis court and slide down the hills and slopes. The idea was to have fun and not get caught by Public Safety, so you had to have skills at riding the tray and being a fast runner in the snow. She never seen so many qualified Olympic runners and tobogganers.

President Reagan was still in office, and times were even more challenging. The popular songs were "**We are the World,**" several artists collaborated on this song, and "**Til, my Baby, Comes Home**" by Luther Vandross. Itchy's mother took out student loans for her to attend college, and she received one Pell Grant for $800; wow. Mom's income was around $18K, not enough to pay for college and too much to qualify for financial aid. The summer program went by fast, and Itchy ended the program with a 2.8 GPA. First-year in college was brutal. Itchy ended up getting pregnant by the boy with jet-black curly hair in high school, he enlisted in the Army in November of 1984, and she was heartbroken.

In 1985 passing the state board exam and becoming a licensed cosmetologist gave Itchy an avenue to make money. While living on campus and during the summer months being able to do hair put extra cash in her pockets. Itchy would faithfully shampoo, press and curl my niece Letreca and cousin Laronda's hair. They both were like her little sisters and very smart, pretty, and innocent little girls. Itchy didn't get to see them as often as in the pass, now it was only on the weekend she would come home. Another time that Itchy was able to spend time with them both and play the older sister role, since Itchy was the youngest child. Every year the University would allow you to bring your little sister or brother on campus for the weekend. Itchy Mae was so excited to have Letreca and Laronda, her niece and cousin ages seven and nine, to stay in the dorm to bring your little sister or brother weekend.

While at Oakland University, Itchy Mae was in OU Gospel Choir. Byron Cage was the Choir Director, and his sister Lynn was one of the lead vocalists. This same year Itchy had the opportunity to meet Oprah Winfrey and hear a phenomenal lecture during Black Awareness Month. It was standing room only during Oprah's speech, and Itchy was right up front, close enough to reach out and touch Oprah at the podium. She also had the pleasure of meeting the comedian Sinbad at OU's Coffee House when he began his comedy career.

During the summer of 1985, Itchy niece Kim moved in, and they had the time of their lives. Her niece taught her to drive. Since age fifteen, Itchy had a driver's permit and feared getting behind the wheel of a car. One day Itchy niece Kim told her it was time for her to learn to drive, and they drove down Plymouth while she was learning to drive. Itchy was so excited that when passing her parents, while stopped at a stop sign and began waving at them. Her niece said, "you are too excited because you don't have license the first and are not even supposed to be driving and you stop and wave at them" Duh! Kim said, "We both are in trouble when we get home, so let's hang out longer and enjoy ourselves."

Later that summer, a concert at *Joe Lewis Arena* featured Run DMC, Whodini & Kool Mo D., and *Aspen Record Shop had a pre-concert party for their fans/groupies.* The record shop was on a Wyoming street, and both groups were there signing autographs and taking pictures.

Itchy and Kim put their cutest matching outfits on and went to *Aspen*, and you will never believe who was selected. They were all set to take pictures with Whodini as long as the line was.

They had their camera, so they asked someone from Whodini's Camp to take their picture, and they began snapping pictures.

The girls left and rushed to get the pictures developed, and when they received the photos back, not one of the pictures came out. They both were so disappointed and just knew they would be able to show all their friends they took pictures with Whodini. Later they found out that there is a way you can make it appear you're taking the photo when only you see the flash. That's when Itchy thought we should have taken the Polaroid camera instead.

It's fall semester and time to see the OU Crew. Christian, LaShawn, Carl, Derrick & Daniel were all thick as thieves in college, hung out daily after their classes, and went to Saga for dinner. During college Itchy had eight close female friends, and three close male friends, Daniel, Derrick, and Carl, which she lost contact with all three. Itchy dated one young man name Jason during her college years that now resides in Arizona, married with two daughters. In later years Christian two sons went to the same school (Burton International) with

Itchy's daughter. The second young lady LaShawn left college in her sophomore year and enlisted in the Army, never to hear from again. Itchy managed to stay in touch with some college friends until this very day; Christian now lives in Atlanta. Verlonda, was Itchy's roommate, for two years, which she saw her in 2007 at Comerica Park at a Tigers Game. She is now married with one daughter.

Itchy sophomore year, she decided to join the first Black Greek female Sorority, Alpha Kappa Alpha Sorority Inc., and after pledging formed a relationship with five more phenomenal women that became sisters. Their line name was 'Intensity Six,' and the pledge period was intense. To no surprise, Itchy Mae was given the nickname 'Ivy Attitude' during the pledge period. After crossing and pledging other prospective ladies, she was referred to as Big Sister Quiet Storm. Again, being the youngest of her line sisters. Two of her Sands live in the suburbs of Georgia, one in Stockbridge, and her twin Sands, that share the same birth date, lives in Lithonia. The other two live in the suburbs of Michigan (Novi & Oak Park), and one lives in Pasenda California. Itchy Mae is still in contact with all five of her line sisters (Sands) until this day.

It took four years to understand and appreciate her mother's wisdom; a mother always knows BEST! Itchy ends up going to college part-time while working full-time at Michigan National Bank and eventually stops going to college altogether.

In 1988 and 1989, Itchy sorority sisters and other friends were graduating with bachelor's Degrees in

Engineering, Nursing, Accounting, Information Systems, Human Services, General Arts, Liberal Arts, and the list goes on.

Now mind you, Itchy had worked two years full-time and was earning about $28K when her peers were making double or even triple her salary after they graduated. A lesson for young people to look at the bigger picture. Don't just live for today; you need to plan for the future, family, rainy days, and retirement years.

CHAPTER THREE

I Married My Blind Date

THE YEAR IS **1989**, and Itchy met her future husband. Itchy had stopped attending college in her junior year and was working two jobs by this time. **Ronald Reagan's** last year in office. The song **"Back to Life" (However, do you want me)** by Soul II Soul was released. It was also the year that the Pistons won the NBA Championship. Itchy was a Bank Teller at Michigan National Bank and drove for a Limousine Company in the evenings. Driving for the limo company all began because of her co-worker. Her co-worker, Charles asked her to go to the Secretary of State with him to get his chauffeur's license. While there, she also took the test and passed it. Charles was eager to get into Corporate America and a graduated from Cass Tech High School in June. He end up becoming like a younger brother and he was in relationship with his high school sweetheart and became like the brother Itchy never had. The young man married his high school sweetheart in 1994. He is a retired Detroit Firefighter, and she is a retired Detroit Police Officer, and they have one daughter and three sons currently living in Brighton, Michigan. He was concerned with Itchy having someone to love because all she did was work, sleep, and hang out sometimes on the weekend.

Charles begins talking about introducing her to his cousin and trying to hook the two of them up to date. By this time, she was ready for a long term committed relationship to settle down. Itchy and Stephanie would hang out on weekends and go on adventures like Thelma and Louise.

For instance, they were hanging out at Palmer Park when the excitement set in after seeing some eye candy pass them on the other side of the road and tried to bust a U-turn. Her friend knocked the car into neutral unknowingly and they thought the car was out of gas when it began moving slowly then stopped. By this time, the guys were gone. Another time they planned a trip to Tennessee to visit their male friends, and this airline seating is first come first serve basis, so to their surprise, their clothes took off in the air, and they were still inside the Southwest City Airport in Detroit. They had to take a taxicab to Metro Airport to fly out on standby. This was Itchy's first time flying, and her friend forgot to get their boarding passes, so when it was time to board the plane, they were sugar honey ice tea out of luck.

Then there was the time they were at Flood's Jazz Club, and Itchy was supposed to be out of town and returned early due to not planning her timing right, so she spent the weekend at her friend house because her parents thought she was out of town. They decided to go out, and while at Flood's, she spotted her sister come into the door. She immediately froze and told her sands they had to squat down and sneak out of the club without being seen. Her friend was so mad at her and said, "I'll be glad when you grow up and get your own place (Itchy is twenty-two now) because we are two grown women ducking and hiding like kids." She goes on to say, "I'm stupid for even letting you convince me to sneak out of a club!"

The last of their adventures is when the two are literally riding on two wheels in a red Dodge Omni. At this time, it was a winter day with snow and ice still in some areas, and they were driving west down I-94 and forgot they needed to merge onto the Lodge Freeway. Itchy accelerated and merged onto the Lodge, entering a ramp with a deep curve. All she remembers is that the car was leaning over to the point that her friend was also holding the steering wheel to help steer and screaming, 'Whatever you do, DON'T put your foot on the brakes!' The two girls were screaming and steering, and when the car finally was on four wheels again in a straight away all was clear, they looked at each other and busted out laughing! These two must thought they were invincible.

The time had come to become more serious about a long-term relationship. Itchy had dated men in town and out of town, so she finally gave in to meet her co-worker's cousin. Little did Itchy know she was about to go on her first blind date. They had talked on the phone and had never met in person. Finally, the evening came; she still lived at home with her parents, so she asked her mother to answer the door. Her mother was appalled that she was going on a blind date! She said, "so when did you get so desperate that you had to go on a blind date?" While trying to explain, the doorbell rings, ding-dong, and her stepfather answers the door. Popa opens the door and says, "it's a little boy at the door." To Itchy surprise, her date sent his cousins teenage brother along and sent him to the door to see how Itchy looked. He instructed his cousin that if Itchy was ugly, to tell her that he couldn't make it and, if she were pretty, to signal him to get out of the car. Mind you this is her co-worker's younger brother at the door. Charles told them that he was not going to tag along as a third wheel.

To make a long story short, he came to the door, and six months later, they were engaged. A year and two months later May 18, 1991, they were married, and they lived a lifestyle like Ike & Tina Turner, but they didn't become known for their singing. Itchy was in denial because she knew he was capable of Domestic Violence (DV) way before they were married. Don't think this can't happen to you. This is not a one-time scenario he has a prior history of DV in other relationships. Make sure you listen intensely when a man speaks and willingly shares intimate encounters in prior relationships. These are red flags and behaviors to beware of such as: wrestling, play fighting, pushing, and choking. These are tested to see how you will react. Let your partner know that all of those forms of contact are outside your boundaries, and these are deal breakers. There are boundaries broken that you clearly stated. Make no exceptions even when you think this won't happen again. Boundary one has been crossed next the person moves in with you after you shared you refuse to shack (live together). Next there is a marriage proposal that you don't take seriously and tell him to stop playing. Later to find out from his mother, he was offended and serious, so you accept. You get a proposal and no ring until he feels you deserves one, six months later. Insecurity sets in you attempt to end the relationship and he comes back. Then a few months after the engagement and announcement they we're getting married, her sister moved to San Antonio Texas and had a going-away party, and Itchy didn't attend. She was so excited about going to her sister's party at *Yesterday's* on Nine Mile Road in Southfield, Michigan. The supposed issue was the outfit selected that was lying on the bed most of the day. It was the cutest purple Bermuda short set with a matching vest with a gold rope chain draped from the buttons with her matching purple sandals. Once she got dressed, He asked her, "where do you think you are going with that on?" This is the beginning of control, isolation and separation from family and friends.

Next thing you know, they are in a drawn-out fight like they were two WWF Wrestlers, and her outfit ends up getting wiped into pieces. They literally had each other in headlocks and fighting onto the bed then onto the floor. Itchy felt horrible and confused. She picked up a long vertical lamp to keep him away from her while threatening to hit him with it if he came closer.

Her sister meant everything to her, but how could she go all bruised up and let her secret get revealed? Itchy knew her family would not tolerate her staying with him, let alone marrying him. Itchy didn't have any brothers, but her sisters would have put a can of whup a$% on him.

Afterwards they would have called the police, something she never did. She felt so much guilt for a few reasons. The first was because her sister had been there and done so much for her. The second reason was Itchy felt like she had failed and would become a disappointment to her family. She held on to hope deferred. In May of 1991, Itchy went ahead with the marriage and kept that secret for many years and experiencing both joy and pain that year. Her favorite uncle Lewis died a month before her wedding at fifty-two years old. That same year in November 1991, her sister Jacquelyn, that moved to Texas, married her long-time sweetheart, and she moved to Herndon, Virginia.

The saying God bless the child that has his own really helps one to understand independence, maturity, and priorities. The pair were young adults neither had lived on their own and left their parent's home to start their own lives. The love of family ran deep to help out because her sister, that moved to Texas, gave the couple all her living room and dining room furniture and helped her various times throughout the years. Booney didn't want any children, and Itchy wanted at least three children. They end up compromising and having their one and only princess. They had some rough times, and they had some beautiful times. They experience close calls like once they were inside Taco Company on Cadieux/ Houston Whittier ordering food and in walks two guys. Booney, said let's go! To my surprise another guy was outside in his trunk getting an automatic weapon out to shoot Booney. We jump into his car and take off down Cadieux in his light blue Merkur XR4Ti and he yells at me saying, "when I say let's go move and don't ask questions." A huge red flag of the pass coming into your current life. On a lighter side of things Itchy and her husband like traveling and visiting states like Ohio, Niagara Falls, Iowa, Virginia, Washington, Arkansas, Chicago, Poconos, New York, and Georgia. They drove to all these places except Niagara Falls. One trip seemed out of a 60's movie, which was unbelievable, is when she visited her friend and husband who lived in Pine Bluff, Arkansas. After returning from a Juke Joint, a police officer pulled them over. And her friend's husband was driving, and when the officer approached the car, he called him boy! He said, "aren't you Mr. Smith, boy?" Then he told him to get out of the car and asked for all of our driver's licenses, then arrested him. The officer took him to the precinct for expired tags on the license plate. Later that night, he released him; however, the officer never mentioned why he stopped us. And this occurred in 1993, and we knew then it was time to get back home to Detroit.

Another trip Itchy enjoyed was when the couple went to the Poconos with her In-laws. They turned from In-Laws into her In-Loves and soon became like second parents. They were close and gave her a lot of guidance as a woman, daughter, and with marriage. Itchy & her husband had never gone on a honeymoon, so his parents arranged for them to go to the Poconos, all expenses paid for, and they had the time of their life. They stayed at one of the exclusive Resorts included horseback riding, paddle boating, putt-putt, skating, and a full-size gym in which the four of them played basketball. Itchy called his Family the Swiss Family Robinson's. They were real outdoor people that loved to swim (except her mother-in-law) and could rough it in a tent and the whole nine.

The first year Itchy was dating Booney is the nickname she gave him. They went to White Cloud near Lake Michigan, camped out in a cabin, and rented 3 - Wheel ATVs, jet skis, and jet boats. She was adventurous but terrified. He had two older brothers, and he, too, was the youngest in his family. Itchy being the daredevil, rode the ATV for the first time and came off a sand dune (taller than the empire state building); her brother-in-law was stuck on the pathway below sand hill between two trees, trying to avoid hitting him, and threw herself off the ATV. Itchy ended up hitting the back of his ATV, ruining the axle, and she flew over the front of her ATV into the sand with branches and tree roots poking out of the ground. Yes, she was okay, but she was fortunate only to break her wrist. That was a light injury from another visiting tourist that had a branch to go clean through his jawbone. Yikes! Many of her friends and family asked if she would do it again, and she told them YES! She felt she was a better rider after that incident and learned some tricks; however, the first year after her accident, she opted for the dune buggy type of ATV that was caged in.

The best way to describe him is that He was handsome, wise, charismatic, and a loving man. He resembled two singers Al B. Sure with a mixture Prince back then. He would do this thing with his lips like Prince, and she would melt. Besides being the youngest child in their family and spoiled, they both had similar issues that stem from their childhood and genetics that they tried to overcome. They were like oil and water; they couldn't mix and formed a 'toxic love and soul tie.'

In **1993** Itchy began mentoring students at Fitzgerald Elementary K-8th Grade. The company she worked for was First of America Bank, and they believed in giving back to the community and allowed the employees to volunteer three hours out of their workday twice a month to help students with reading and math.

Itchy also began volunteering at Salvation Army Girls Home as well where she ended up meeting a young lady that was like a ray of light and full of ambition. By coincidence, she had the same name as her sister. This young lady became her God sister and was like a little Angel, and things turned around for her positively, and until this very day, they are still close as ever. She is a Pharmacist Technician at DMC Hospital, married with one son and a baby girl on the way.

This is also the year Itchy had a miscarriage and thought she was unable to have children because she did not have a child in 1984 and it haunted and depressed her for years. Itchy asked God for forgiveness, although she had never completely forgiven herself.

Itchy didn't have a relationship with her dad after graduating from high school until her adult life. Her dad attended the wedding in 1991; however, they didn't talk regularly. Booney named their daughter Makayla, and it was his idea for their daughter to get to know her maternal grandfather better and to introduce him to his new granddaughter. To both their surprise, in March of

1996, the couple welcomed their one and only Princess into the world.

In 1996 Itchy Mae called her dad to tell him about his new grandchild, and from that day forward, they became closer than close. He calls Itchy a jive turkey and she calls him her gentle giant, and her daughter calls him Big Daddy. As for Booney, he was wise in saying that they shouldn't have any more children. Itchy felt that was selfish when he was utilizing his wisdom, which saved her from a future struggle she would later encounter with her daughter's behavior.

In terms of coping with being married and living in a domestic violent marriage it was key to keep a job and stay physically healthy with strength training. Either before or after work Bally's is like a second home. In 1998 Itchy had the opportunity to meet another Piston Player, Joe Dumar, which she had a crush on Joe Dumar's growing up and had met him along with many of the Pistons players like John Sally, Rick Mahorn, and Vinnie at the famous Maxi's Night Club in Detroit back in 1987-1989. Seeing Joe was different this time, more on a professional basis. Being the VP Buyers Executive Administrator of a Plastics Company called Textron Automotive and in attendance at a meeting that Joe Dumar's Company gave a presentation when he first ventured into the Tier II Automotive Business.

Booney was raised as a Jehovah's Witness and didn't celebrate holidays. Itchy planned her husband a surprise 30th birthday party in 2000, his first official birthday party. The party was at Nichols Night Club in Southfield,

Michigan. He had the time of his life and danced all night, and a videographer captured the event and made a video to music, 'All I do is think about you' by Stevie Wonder.

The following year 2001 marked the completion of bachelor's degree in Business Management from the University of Phoenix -Troy while working full-time, being married, and raising her one and only princess. Her husband planned a fabulous graduation party at Mountain Jacks, and her parents and all her siblings and their families and Godmother Gracie helped celebrate. This was an enormous step for Booney because he shared that he felt like she cheated on him with her job and education. His fear stem from the higher Itchy advanced herself that she would want to leave him and marry someone that worked in Corporate America (white collar) that Itchy had more in common with her. Regarding their marriage, they were together for sixteen years including married and separations for thirteen years. They tried to stay together by seeking marriage counseling and talking to Elders, Itchy's Pastor, going on couple retreats, psychiatrist and seeing a therapist Savannah Woods.

Itchy loved him dearly and valued her married, so she didn't continue her education after getting a Bachelor's. He had even threatened that he would divorce her if she pursued a master's degree. He felt like she put those things before him and made him feel insecure. They trouble bonded with one another and shared many deep secrets from their childhood, tween years and teenage years. Therefore, she was afraid to leave him because he used those things to manipulate her to stay. Divorce was used as a threat and never put into action only to control. Other clear signs of blame, guilt, and dependency that a person uses against you in domestic violent relationship.

The lesson learned was to accomplish your goals because you may regret it later or not live long enough to reach your goals. Also, never think you can change a man. Believe him when he tells you who he is because he will change you and have you lost and turned out! The saying equally yoked means more than being the same religious denomination. It also deals with having similar desires regarding education, having children, being married, or living together, short, and long-term goals, fears, weaknesses, and strengths. Other than money, sex, and religion, several things need to get discussed when selecting a companion. You may think you know a person and find out you don't once you live with them. You need to ask about their childhood. What happen bad and good in their childhood? What are their morals and beliefs and what are their deal breakers?

Itchy Mae always enjoyed going to concerts out of town, for instance, the Cincinnati Jazz Festival, and in town at Venues like the Pine Knob/DTE, Palace, Meadowbrook, Freedom Hill, the Fox & most of all, Chene Park. She saw some of the best performances at Chene Park with plentiful seating. I had the opportunity to meet Will Downing and Chante Moore but had to decline to go backstage because Booney was acting uncomfortable and insecure. Both vocalists were very humble and down-to-earth individuals. Itchy remember having backstage passes but giving them away to my cousin Kim and her son Sean. She played it cool and opted not to go backstage to avoid a verbal or physical fight in public. Another clear sign of DV when a person is willing to pick a fight in public over their insecurity. There were two men that Itchy was crazy about, and He despised it, and that was Will Downing and Michael Jordan. It was something about a tall, dark, bald man that just tickled her fancy.

After two reconciliations, they finally divorced in October 2004, which is also recognized as domestic violence (DV) month. Until this very day, Itchy Mae considers her ex-husband a good co-parent from her perspective. Her daughter view is totally different, and she is lack luster about their visits. Just because the marriage didn't work doesn't make him bad man; it means he was not the loving man to Itchy. They will always love one another and agreed to raise their beloved daughter together. Even though they could not make it together, it didn't stop them from raising their daughter together. The lesson learned was Forgiveness!

In 2002 Itchy took a new outlook on life when she began praying regularly and developed a closer relationship with God. That same year she heard the song 'Smile' by the late Tupac Shakur, and she knew it was better to smile no matter how bad life's trials were because you could be worse off or dead. When Itchy was a child, her aunt Toosie always told her to stop frowning so much and smile. My aunt was right; it takes thirteen muscles to smile and forty-seven to frown.

2002 was also when Stephanie, Regina-Sister Soldier, and Itchy Mae began taking their Sabbatical for a three to five-day getaway. Sister Soldier was given this name not for being radical or activist; however, she served her country by fighting in The Gulf War & Desert Storm. Sister Soldier is a Florida Police Officer by day and has been in the Army Reserves for 25 years. My Sands, Stephanie is a Social Worker for the State of Michigan. All three women are divorced women raising children, so they agreed to meet every other year and have girl's time full of fun, sun, and relaxation. The first trip was to Vegas, Florida, Myrtle Beach, ATL, Chicago, and the Bahamas. They were raising preteens, teenagers, and young adults and decided everyone needs 'Me Time' and 'Adult Time,' you better embrace it whenever the opportunity arrives.

The year that Kwame Kilpatrick was elected the youngest black mayor of Detroit and served office from January 1, 2002, and resigned on September 4, 2008, after many scandals and a guilty plea to two felonies. Yes, Itchy voted for the youngest mayor this first term and had the opportunity to meet him at one of the Taste Festival held in the New Center of Detroit.

CHAPTER FOUR

The Humbling Year

THE YEAR IS 2006, It was the first week of January and was devastated because Itchy had only been without a job for one week. Itchy Mae was a contract employee at Daimler Chrysler in Auburn Hills at the time and received notice that the assignment was over after four years. She tried not to carry this bad news on the trip and waited until afterward to share the information. Itchy's mother, three sisters, and went to Phoenix, Arizona, to participate in a half marathon. It was her sister's idea, who had run in two marathons before this in Arizona and Bermuda. Itchy her sister, and mom walked the thirteen-mile event for Heart & Stroke Association, while her other two sisters were their cheerleaders. The three finished in three and a half hours. Itchy was now thirty-nine and had been working since she was fifteen years old, her first was a job working at Michigan Osteopathic Hospital as a student dietitian. Itchy was devastated because she had only been without a job for one week. She was a contract employee at Daimler Chrysler in Auburn Hills at the time and received notice that her assignment was over after four years. Itchy tried not to carry this bad news with her on the trip, so she waited until afterward to share the information.

Itchy had worked in the Banking Industry for thirteen years and left First of America Bank once they merged with National City Bank. She reinvented herself by learning Microsoft Excel, PowerPoint & Access and changed to a different career field, the Automotive Industry. Itchy went to a contract house in Dearborn, Michigan, that only placed workers with the Big Three or Tier II Suppliers. Itchy took all types of tests to get her administrative skills above requirements, started working in the Purchasing Department, and then moved into the Engineering & Design Department. Later, she gaining automotive experience working at Textron Automotive began working as a contract employee at Daimler Chrysler in their IT Department. Itchy returned and placed her resume with hundreds of companies. She had several interviews and finally landed a job in September of that year. During those eight months, Itchy Mae learned that pride only gets you further in debt and deeply depressed. As Itchy mother had told her, she also learned to slow down so many times before.

After my unemployment benefits ended in August 2006, no extensions were approved. Itchy was praying for a job and had decided that if she didn't get a job by November, they would relocate to Lithonia, Georgia, and move in with her Sorority Sister (Twin Sands). Her sister Jacqueline that lived in Connecticut at the time called in a favor from a long-time college friend that owned her own Contract Company. The plan was to work at a Wireless Company in Clinton Township as a contract employee. By this time, bills were behind and piling up. Itchy had to swallow her pride and ask family members and her ex-husband for help. At this point, Itchy felt as though she had hit rock bottom! Her ex-husband paid her car payment for three months, and her mother, sisters, in-laws, friends, and members of her congregation also helped.

Experiencing life without a job after the contract position ended at Daimler Chrysler. Itchy Mae pride was in the way and her heat was shut off due to no payment. Itchy's ex-husband extended the invite for Itchy and their daughter to stay at his apartment. Itchy was uncomfortable staying at his place due to him having a girlfriend and didn't want the drama. Fortunately, she humbled herself and asked her sister for the money to get the heat reconnected. Itchy decided to stay at her dad's house since they were going out of town for a week and her dad asked her to house sit.

On November 27, 2006, Itchy Mae began a new job training at a Sub Prime Auto Lender where she landed a direct-hire job. Several lessons were engraved in her mind. One was to make sure you save money for at least six months to a year of a separate savings in case of emergency. The second lesson 'Pride is before a crash' is when a person's intellectual side prevails over them using common sense. When in reality at some point in every person's life you're going to need help from someone, and a quiet mouth doesn't get fed. The following year in 2007

Itchy's life changed tremendously in ways Mary J. Blige's chart-topping songs, going from 'My Life' to 'Just Fine".

Being from the 'Motor City' Itchy always loved cars, especially sports cars and high-performance cars with speed. Itchy love to see how fast her 1998 green Camaro, six-speed stick shift could go on I-696 heading eastbound into the I-94 curve down shifting with confidence. Itchy loved to run and was trying to play catch up on every opportunity she thought she had missed out on. Speaking of running Itchy Mae admired the late 'Flo Jo' Florence Griffith – Joyner, which is still considered the "fastest running woman of all time" 100 meters (10.49). She also had the desire to become a racecar driver and admired Danica Patrick the fourth woman racecar driver to compete in the Indianapolis 500 and posted the "fastest practice speed" years later she goes on to become the first woman to win an Indy 500 race. The Moral or lesson here is there is a time and place for everything and sometimes speeding doesn't help you to win, although endurance at a steady pace qualifies as a win.

THE WAY I BEHAVE

The way I behave
Is not to seek mine but
Another Glory.
The way I behave
Is to tell my life story
The way I behave
Is like a book a child can read
The way I behave
A message of hope for others
To receive.
The way I behave
Just might rescue someone's life
The way I behave
Could save another misery and strife
The way I behave
I let my life so shine
The way I behave
Always leaving joy and happiness behind
The way I behave
I hope will follow behind me
The way I behave
A highway of peace and kindness
The way I behave
My purpose told so well
The way I behave
To deliver just one soul from hell
The way I behave

When this world I depart
The way I behave
Loving God and my neighbor with
All my heart

Author: Rev. Caleb B. Gardner

CHAPTER FIVE

Eyes Wide Open

THIS PART OF the story is about Itchy Mae's 'Mini-Me.' Itchy's life story would not be complete if she did not mention her Darling Daughter. When her daughter was born, the light bulb came on, and she could not walk around with her eyes closed shut any longer. The first year of her life was a blessing and a wisdom walk. Itchy wanted the best for her child like any other mother and tried to raise her in a two-parent household. After she turned six months, her husband decided to move out to find himself; he stated, 'he had to decide what he would do with his life." Itchy thought to herself, what perfect timing would he decide to leave us now? The year is September 1996 when they separated, and he moved in with his older brother. He was having an affair with a woman he worked with at Mark IV Manufacturing Plant. Itchy found the woman's picture hidden in a welding book that he would study to prepare for a test. Itchy did not have any desire to raise her daughter alone. After three months, Itchy, asked him to come back home so they could raise their daughter together.

To give you a little background about Itchy Mae ex-husband, he came from a two-parent home, and his parents are still together and celebrating their 50th Anniversary in 2011. Her mother was married to her dad for twenty-one years, later marrying her stepfather and becoming a widow. Itchy's dad remarried twice after his first marriage. Itchy desire was for her daughter to have her father in the home. Itchy also did not desire to have children with another man however, Booney had a vasectomy six months after the birth of their child. Itchy didn't want to repeat a cycle of divorce. Life is funny and requires wisdom because at what cost do you determine rather it is healthier, helping or hurting your child to leave or stay? Itchy Mae's husband came back home, and the same old things went on before the child was born with the verbal and physical abuse. That led this time for her to move out in 2001, so she would not send the wrong message to her daughter that abusive behavior is acceptable. At that time, Itchy also placed a police protective order on him. A year later, Itchy returned to try this thing called marriage once again and live up to her vows, for better or for worse. They decided to focus on their daughter when she returned home, that was something they agreed on. She also had the police protective order removed from his record. This is when Itchy's Mae prayer life became stronger, reading the Bible and going to Bible Study. There is a scripture 1 Corinthians 10:13 "God is faithful he will provide a way out."

Their daughter started in Montessori School in St Claire Shores, Michigan. They wanted the best education for her, as most parents desire. Then they thought it didn't make sense to pay college tuition for a child in Preschool and Kindergarten, so they changed her school to Edison

Academy for first grade, a charter school in Detroit, Michigan. Again, they still wanted better, and some of the things discussed when we were accepted, such as your child having their own laptop changed our minds. The school did provide the laptops; however, it was for students in the fourth through eighth grades. We began looking at the top three public schools of choice in Detroit: Bates Academy, FLIC Emerson & Burton International. Both her parents attended public schools in Detroit, Michigan, and so can their daughter. After interviewing with the principal and administrative staff, Burton International gave a letter of acceptance. She attended Burton from second through fifth grade, and the school went to the eighth grade.

Detroit schools had been deteriorating for quite some time. That was the point of naming all the schools to emphasize the education system. Our daughter never attended the neighborhood school on the east side of Detroit due to class size. There were thirty-five to forty students in some classrooms. We are aware of the wars in other countries, but many people don't know about the war right here in our central city. Teachers and Parents were fed up and waiting on something to be done about the lack of books, supplies, desks, resources, and support from the state. Many residents left the city due to education and city services in Detroit, Michigan. Teachers were underpaid and had an additional 10% deducted from their paychecks.

Itchy's daughter was not an angel and is the typical teenager with issues of peer pressure, boys, dating, Facebook, playing sports, and shopping to get the hottest/ latest clothing. She likes (True Religion, Joe's & Mek

Jeans, Hollister, Abercrombie & Fitch) and the list goes on. Itchy had to share the logical way of thinking with her daughter about clothing. For example, she taught her to buy the traditional clothing that doesn't go out of style. You can wear year after year and still be in style with designers like Ralph Lauren/ Polo, Levi Jeans, Old Navy & Gap Clothing. They have been around for a long time and are always in style. The high-ticket price name brands are stylish, but there is a new designer every couple of years that stays around long enough for the consumer to buy the latest designer's clothing. Explaining to her daughter that the parents who can afford the name brands don't buy them for their children; it's the lower to middle-class parents purchasing them. Itchy also explained to look at the parents that can't afford to buy groceries and gas and pay their bills on time and don't have any money saved in the bank. Itchy emphasized to her daughter that your education, savings account, and good credit will take you a long way! Itchy always thought if the money we are paying to clothe our children goes to educate them with good books, computers, and resources, our children would become extraordinary individuals. We wouldn't need the lottery to give a portion to help the school districts.

Itchy's daughter had an economic course this trimester, and she had to teach her a lesson that she learned almost too late about the economy and the consumer. Itchy Mae had her first MasterCard in college by the time she was eighteen. Itchy also incurred student loan debt that she didn't think anything about while in college. My point to my daughter is that most young adults start in debt before they graduate from college, which is why she emphasize scholarships.

The fact that you may dress in all the latest designer clothing and don't own it is because you must pay back the money to your creditor. Lots of people buy on impulse and don't think of the consequences. American Express was the only credit card company for years that required you to pay for what you purchased. Within the last decade, they have set up different credit accounts modeled after the traditional credit card companies (buy now, pay later). Believe me. Itchy have purchased enough wisdom to own a small island. She explained to her that the economy was on a downward spiral because the consumers that were buying did not have good credit or strong credit. These individuals are lower and middle-class Americans. In the African American community, we learned to own something is more important than what you are wearing. Those that know better do better and question those priorities that prefer to invest their money in cars, clothing, and jewelry over owning a home. There's a saying that you have on everything you own.

Our society has been allowed to buy homes, and luxury cars that we would have not qualified for in the past. Banking Institution required a 740-credit score, or Mortgage Company would not lend to Black & Brown people in the past. People were spending money they didn't have and accepting any ARM or APR to get into a house. Now the city of Detroit is being abandoned due to education and city services declining. The majority of individuals still living in Detroit own their homes or inherited the house from a deceased relative, and people ask them why they stay? They stay because the all-American dream of freedom of choice and speech! Whatever happen to lay-a-way from back in the good old days? Our society needs to wake up because it is nothing worse than owning nothing and owing creditors. There is a little-known cliche, "you don't have a pot to piss in or a window to throw it out of!"

In recent years TJ Maxx, Burlington Coat Factory, K-Marts, and a few other department stores may have this, but some get insulted when you say lay-of-way. It is a possibility that's why several K-Marts have closed, due to the competitors selling designer brands. Shop now and pay later. Itchy explain to her daughter what happened to the housing market and the Big Three during 2007-2008. Living in Michigan, believe me, we saw it at its worst. Jobs were outsourced, which is a horrible combination. You don't need a degree in economics to observe this. Just keep living, as my mother would say. There was no money being put back into the economy. We now have Rent a Center to rent furniture and electronics, and then we have places in urban neighborhoods that rent rims. Payday Advance companies within every two to three miles. All the banks and mortgage companies did was let you put your house in the layaway, and when you couldn't make the payments, they restocked your home (foreclosure), and you didn't get your deposit back. In essence, the layaway theory helps you spend less and live within your means. Itchy Mae was not a frugal person; however, she changed her spending habits to survive during the gas and grocery price increase.

Academically she deserves the credit for being an outstanding student; she was in the National Junior Honor Society and Great Lakes Scholars until the eighth grade. She also attended two other schools, one being Roosevelt Middle School in Oak Park, Michigan, for sixth and seventh grades, which was closer to my job. This school was a suburban school that offered open enrollment to other communities.

After reminiscing, Itchy noticed her neighborhood changing back in 2000, and in 2007 after being divorced for three years, Itchy decided to move outside Detroit into a suburb. Her daughter could get a better education to prepare her for college, especially after her daughter share that she wanted to become a cardiovascular surgeon.

Itchy has grand ambitions and goals and encourages her daughter that it is good to dream; however, when we think great, we become great and turn a dream into a reality. Her daughter attended the eighth grade at Power Middle School in Farmington Hills, Michigan, where her class was the last middle school class to graduate from that school due to school closings. The state of Michigan is now experiencing school closings in all counties. Itchy's daughter is currently in high school, and they have her preparing for her ACT Exams with a company called Exam Experts. The company owner recommends that students take the test five times before submitting their final scores to their university of choice.

My decision to focus on my daughter's education is crucial because she is fortunate to have her dad's good test-taking skills and reading comprehension. Itchy must acknowledge her daughter's dad because he has been a visible and good father, and the media often talk about African American men that abandon their children. I want to give credit when credit is due! Real talk, many of my close friends who have gone through a divorce or had children are raising their children alone. Her dad stepped up to the plate and hit a home run. He plays, studies (helps with school science projects), and nurtures her every other weekend and during the summers because Itchy is the custodial parent. The bottom line is that most parents would like their children to have better than they did. Itchy Mae tried to set her daughter up for success. She started by making sure her weaknesses were her daughters strengths. Itchy taught her daughter not to let anyone break her self-esteem, not to accept abusive behavior, and not to say, "I'm sorry!"

We are not sorry, people; however, we will apologize, and we do forgive.

Enrolling Makayla in ballet classes for poise and gracefulness was also to expose her to other children being the only child. Itchy daughter told her, "Mom I don't like dancing on my toes", so she switched her into tumbling and gymnastics at age three instead of ballet. I had a fear of swimming (Itchy didn't learn until she was fourteen), so; Itchy started her swimming lessons at the age of four at Coleman A. Young Center in Detroit, Michigan, and she started as a tadpole and now swims like a fish. Reflecting back, Itchy lacked rhythm and couldn't make the cheer team. Makayla made a minor league team- Falcons, elementary and high school cheer team.

Another one of Itchy's fears was driving as a teenager, so Itchy and her husband allowed her to drive before going to driver's training. Itchy was an average student with a grade point average of 2.5 –3.0, so Itchy read to her at night starting at three months and played classical music while she slept, and she maintained a 3.5 - 4.0 grade point average until eighth grade and now holds a 3.4-grade point average. She's learned three languages, Spanish, Japanese & German, and she is most familiar with Spanish. The year her daughter was born, Itchy opened her a savings account at the credit union, at age fourteen she opened a checking account with a debit card.

In order to teach money management, she opened her daughter a teenage checking account that was linked to a debit card, so once the money is gone, the spending stops (buy and pay now). She was amazed to see me write out a check, and asked what is that because her generation was more familiar with a debit or ATM Card. Another piece of wisdom she shared to remain abstinent and wait to have sex once she's married, unlike Itchy did. Last and not least Itchy laid a strong foundation for believing and trusting in God and his son Jesus Christ. Proverbs 3:5 says trust in God with all your heart and **not** lean upon your understanding. She think that she prepared the way for her daughter to succeed and laid a foundation of bricks, so thank God she has achieved all she has at this point in her life, and she look forward to watching her become a phenomenal young woman. The best way to illustrate this reminds me of Billie Holiday's song goes, "God Bless the Child" which got their own.

CHAPTER SIX

Invisible

DEALING WITH ANXIETY and depression is difficult and sometimes you want to disappear, so you don't have to face your reality. Anxiety causes you to worry about things like, do others know all your issues, or do others realize you are at your wits end. If not, careful you can develop impulsive spending habits. Another reaction staying busy with nervous energy with frequent racing thoughts. Then you spiral and your body shuts you down during the time of depression causing you to sleep a lot and when you wake up you still face the same issues. Most times pouring time and energy into others to avoid the trauma of the past or current issues that causes the anxiety. The learned behavior was to pray about it and wait for God to fix it. The Bible scripture Philippians 4:6-7 "Be anxious for nothing, but in everything by prayer and supplication, with thanksgiving let your request be made known to God; and the peace of God, which surpasses all understanding, will guard your hearts and minds through Christ Jesus."

Now religion is a very touchy subject and has been debated, researched, and scrutinized for centuries. There are over four thousand religions globally, and new ones are steadily evolving. Itchy Mae is a Christian as thirty-one percent of people are in the world and believe in God, whose name is Jehovah, and his son Jesus Christ, and the Holy Spirit is our helper. Being a Christian is a challenging walk-in life and things don't become easier. You will experience trials and tribulations in your life that you ask why me? Keep serving God! Why not you? Just think of Jesus Christ, who died for all our sins and had to suffer, tortured, shamed, and humiliated, don't expect anything less as an imperfect human. Humans are so judgmental and condemning, and Jesus walked the earth for 33 ½ years so we could reconcile our relationship with God our Heavenly father.

A song by the Gospel Artist Kierra Sheard called 'Invisible' best explains this chapter of the book. My plight is to encourage anyone that reads this book to believe and trust in God, and he will accept you! God is headlining this chapter of the book and each new chapter of my life. For God's son, a perfect man who came and died for all mankind's sins. He knows our troubles, and why we suffer, he does not cause the suffering! You can accept Jesus by repeating these words. "Dear Lord Jesus, I know I am a sinner, and ask for your forgiveness. I believe that you died for my sins and rose from the dead. I turn from my sins and invite You to come into my heart and life. I want to trust and follow You as my Lord and Savior".

God gives us the 'Free Will' to serve him and is allowing us the time to choose him; however, we must go to God through Jesus Christ. Jesus is the one that reconciled our relationship with God after our first parents, Adam, and Eve were thrown out of the Garden of Eden, that which we inherited our sins. The "Spiritual War" going on for centuries is between God & Satan. God allows us to be tested only to prove that we are not designed to serve him, and we do so on our own 'Free Will". God does not kill children to allow them to go to heaven to be with him. He is not a cruel or unjust God. All that is born will die, and rest in our graves until Jesus returns, and we will hear the sound of his voice and be judged, John 5: 28-29. Without further delay, I would like to introduce to some and make known to many my Heavenly Father God.

Nothing is *absolute* in life other than you will live and die and that Jehovah God created the world and all humankind. Everyone believes in their religion/ denomination and God is superior to all other gods. Some religions question whether Jesus was the Messiah or a prophet. The Bible and Jesus life story his testimony and legacy. This sequel proves evidence of a strong faith and trust in Jesus. Itchy Mae is a living testimony in sound mind, good health and can leave her daughter this inheritance. Itchy have never left God, and God will never leave her. When going through trials and tribulations Itchy would study the Bible more, drawing closer to God and attend church regularly never isolating myself. This is a public declaration that I love Jehovah God, Jesus Christ & The Holy Spirit. God was waiting for me to humble myself from this whole charade of being the headliner on stage. All the Glory belongs to God. Itchy made a religious transition from being Baptist and converting to becoming one of Jehovah's Witnesses from 2004-to 2008. Itchy realized then that she feared God who sees all that she does more than man. You do not have to confess your sins to an imperfect man, just to GOD. Itchy Mae left the JW Faith in 2008 and began visiting New Hope Missionary Baptist Church and later joining New Hope Missionary Baptist Church in January 2011.

One may ask why the drastic change in religions. The decision to begin a regular Bible study with Jehovah's Witness in 2002 was first to save her marriage and keep the family together upon returning home, to reconcile with her husband, they began studying together. This end up being another manipulative move on his part because he had begun another affair with a woman, he worked with at Chrysler this time and he was leading a double life, that he thought Itchy was unaware of.

The most important thing to remember is not to do something just because most of society is but based on purpose. As Christians, we must watch out for distractions! Follow your gut feeling which is the Holy Spirit helping you. When you read and study the Bible there is a discernment you develop. About two decades ago, there was a well-known slogan (What Would Jesus Do?); people sold items with this slogan; however, Jesus is NOT for sale and he can't be bought. Jesus bought the ransom for our sins, and God gives us the 'Free Will' to serve him or not serve him. We are all imperfect humans on this planet called Earth.

In closing, Now is the opportunity to witness to many and share a favorite scripture found in

1 Corinthians 9:27 "I discipline my body like an athlete, training it to do what it should. Otherwise, I fear that after I have preached to others, I might be disqualified." Itchy Mae prayer is that her name will be written in God's Book of Life. There is one God and one Truth, all humans will live, die, and bow down before God. You have the 'Free Will' to choose.

CHAPTER SEVEN

A Few Good Men

NOW ITCHY WAS a hopeless romantic and the men she attracted were a toss between good and questionable. Later learning that these men mirror her traits of abandonment, brokenness, health fanatic, driven, happy and enjoy dancing, etc. Now the movie, "For Colored Girls" explains a lot about her life. Itchy's relationships were like several of the characters' life experiences in the film except for two. Itchy thought that sex was the way to show a man she loved and cared about him. Itchy felt that she was sharing her precious goods with a man and there was power in intimacy that would make a man fall in love with you. Wrong! This stems from daddy issues and not having the close relationship with her father as a child. A father's love is usually the first man a little girl is exposed to love and admire as her provider and protector.

Coming from a woman who had experience traumatic situations from childhood of being groomed and fondled. Later in her adult life, she was shot at while living in the well-known Apartments in Downtown Detroit, by her fiancé's ex-girlfriend. Her husband put a gun to her head to come back home after attempting to divorce him in the first year of marriage and still living to tell this story. Itchy later found that she was giving away her power and becoming a dumping ground. Itchy now knows where her ability is, and it's not between her thighs. The emphasis is on prayer, therapy, and self-evaluation., which makes a miraculous difference in her life.

There is also power in semen, and it can create a life or destroy a life. Semen is also powerful enough to cause a spirit of confusion. It can also pass on a disease or infection! There is instruction in the Bible 1 Corinthians 6:18 that says flee from fornicating. Every other sin a man may commit is outside his body, but he that practices fornication is sinning against his own body. God's guidance against fornication is to **prevent** you from many problems. Sex is meant to be shared among a husband and wife during sex, because you become one not only in body but also in soul. For instance, every time you have sex with a man without using a condom (which is dangerous), his semen flows into your body, and few particles, or hormones may enter into your bloodstream. A deposit is made. Now this deposit consists of **everyone** he's had sex with, which can affect you on a physical and spiritual basis. On the other hand, each time a man enters a woman's vagina he too is entering where other men have gone before. Then soul ties are developed, and you have to break it by never sleeping with them again and removing yourself from their life.

See, life is funny because it will have you upside down and turned inside out if you let it! Some women think they are getting turned out. The real deal is you're getting turned into a dumping ground. We all understand that a man needs to release, but don't become his dumping ground. Before you open those thighs and begin to lust, think about all the trash, and burdens you will have to carry inside you. Open your eyes. You can have intimacy with a man without having sexual relationship.

A man that loves and cares about you can wait and will wait. In the instance he does not wait the rejection is your projection. As women, we need to set boundaries and learn to dismiss the desires and ideas that a man doesn't want to be with you if you don't have sex with him. Many times, you can have sex with a man, and he still does the disappearing act and on to the next. This can work both ways with a woman ghosting a man when she has baggage, hurt people hurt others.

Starting with the man that got away went into the Navy in 1987, this was a gentleman that wanted to marry Itchy, and she was young and afraid. Itchy went to high school with him and reconnected with him at St. Andrews in Greek Town at a Greek Party while home from college. They started dating in the summer of 1986. He, too, was athletic and was on the swim team when they were in high school and a good man. Itchy was very close with his parents, and his sisters and his loving mother died after battling Cancer.

Then there was the man who cared enough making her honorable in God's eyes and asked for Itchy hand in marriage for 13 years. They co-parent their one and only princess. He was very adventurous, attractive, fun, and enjoyed reading and encouraged her to read, Terry

McMillan's book 'Waiting to Exhale" together. He also emphasized learning how to balance everything going on in life and told me to stop trying to please everyone and make myself happy.

Next, it was the gentleman she dated two years after her divorce that she found a true friend; they both were contract employees at Daimler Chrysler, and their daughters have the same name. They both knew they were not ready for marriage, so they parted. After moving to Michigan for his career, he returned to Rochester, New York.

There was indeed a dedicated young man that Itchy dated in her twenties that later moved to Oklahoma and acquired a bachelor's degree in Theology and became a Pastor. He contacted her in their forties to rekindle the relationship while desiring to take a wife. With so much hurt and disappointment from a prior relationship Itchy was not ready to become any ones wife. It was time for more self-evaluation and time to heal.

Then there is the man who lived in the neighborhood that enjoyed jogging and found it spiritually gratifying to admit he wasn't ready for a sexual relationship or marriage.

Itchy was shocked and questioned this man's sexuality and asked him if he was on the down low.

Never did it cross her mind just to become his friend because, at this time, she had been abstinent for three years. He complimented her discipline to follow God's instruction, and she questioned his manhood. Wow what a double standard that she didn't recognize until later, she still maintained a friendship and occasionally had lunch with him.

Then there was a gentleman that brought life and balances back into Itchy's life. This particular man was her movie, dance, exercise, and skating buddy. He had been divorced for eighteen years and learned to enjoy life and not focus so much on having a relationship, sex, and getting re-married. He was confident and could ballroom dance, hustle, an overall good dancer. He hung out at Yesterday at its new location on Telegraph. Itchy met him once at Yesterday's and danced the night away. The club scene was no longer her forte but exercising and skating consumed much of her time.

Also, the gentleman who lived in the same complex in Farmington Hills would work out together at Powerhouse Gym on Halsted. It was nothing for them to hang out at a friend's pool party or the local Sports Bar playing pool. They would have a great time together, especially when he would do his famous Teddy Pendergrass Performance and would honestly give a good Concert.

Her Muse is what he was to me. He was her first, and she intended him to become my last because he loved me first. We reunited after twenty-nine years at our all-class high school reunion. Itchy thought he was the one and became intimidated when he didn't see that she was the Prize and he considered himself the prize. Itchy Mae grew impatient because he was not ready to marry me after three years of a committed relationship. He was divorced always talked about getting married again He said, "He was not going to play married." Later Itchy discovered he would marry again but not her. Itchy was delusional and ended the relationship and entered another relationship with a man ready to get married after seven months of dating; however, she was still in love with my Muse. She ended the relationship after nine months and realized it was her that wasn't ready to become a wife and get married. Her Muse asked her to come back to him, and he told her to stop this "Insanity." Evidently a few months later he gets married to someone else and shares the information with Itchy a year later. Through all the connections, she learned to be enough loving herself.

Once in a lifetime, a Prince comes along into a woman's life. Then you hear from God telling you to be still and wait, because the timing may not present itself, so you should continue to listen to God and not your heart or pride. It is wiser to keep gleaming in the field while waiting on the Lord by being a virtuous woman. Itchy's daddy often quoted the bible scripture about being a virtuous woman. She referred to her dad as a gentle giant, being the first man, she loved in her life.

One of the main common denominators in the relationships is the woman in the mirror needed to heal. Another common factor with all these friendships and relationships there were no regrets. It's just the romantic side that yearns to be loved. Janet Jackson's famous song "That's the way love goes" is a good description. After learning to embrace the good times, lessons learned, and the fact of the matter is each person is responsible for their own happiness when you are single or married.

MY LOVE

My love is too unique to beseech and leaves me with a feeling of being complete. Beneath all things we gain from a woman's unclaimed stories, we will not be ashamed because life stories can help heal another sister's pain!

Author: Joi C. Spencer

CHAPTER EIGHT

The Year Itchy Died

THE YEAR HAD come and gone, and it was December 30, 2010, and Itchy had gotten so depressed that she just wanted to die! Itchy fought with depression most of her adult life and tried hiding it from others. Only Itchy's dad, and oldest sister, knew to a certain degree. Itchy had seen therapists and psychiatrists but was never diagnosed with any chemical imbalance. The doctors would tell her that things that happened to her as a child and during her marriage were traumatic, and she never healed. The first psychiatrist Itchy saw was during her freshmen year in high school when she was fourteen. Itchy had to go to summer school because she skipped Algebra, English and Typing class in her freshmen year and had low grades for her final report card marking. At the end of summer school, she received A's in both classes. Another lesson learned not to skip class to dumb yourself down to hang out in the lunchroom.

Her mother arranged a visit to a psychiatrist on Wayne States Campus. Itchy's behavior had changed, and her mother wanted her evaluated after becoming very defiant and began skipping school and disrespectful to adults. Itchy never shared much with the psychiatrist, and she just watched the time go by on the clock. She had no plans to share that she was being groomed or fondled for years. Itchy talked to her imaginary friends aloud and openly when at home to cope with. During Itchy's childhood and tween years, she began talking to her imaginary friends while playing with toys, which later became her safe space to zone out of the real world to survive the grooming.

She was deceptive and told her mother about having a summer job with the City of Detroit as a student landscaper. Not until recently, Itchy's mother still didn't know she had never worked that summer job.

Now by age twenty the attention to cope led to looking for love in relationships with men that she could nurture or fix. Another way she managed anxiety was by mentoring other young girls or women that had experienced similar issues. Getting back to the night, Itchy was so depressed. Itchy kept crying and just wanted the sadness to end! Yes, she now had a teenage daughter that lived with her, with whom she shared joint custody with her ex-husband, and this was the weekend her daughter was at home with her.

On that very night, Itchy decided it was time to end it, and that is when she decided to end her life! Itchy knew it had gone on far too long and had to kill herself. So, at that very moment, she grabbed her Bible and began to pray to God to keep her mind and let the little girl go away and her past, her insecurities and the imaginary friends go away. Itchy finally learned to let the scared little girl die and let the Godly woman live that she had become. The best way to describe how she felt is stated best in the well-known song by Tina Turner in 1962 and the remake

Keyshia Cole made in 2009, "Make Me Over." You see, Itchy was too selfless and clever to commit suicide, and she knew it was not going to be a physical death but a figurative one. In the rare instance of being selfish, Itchy couldn't commit suicide because she had work to do to help others.

Her life story is more significant than you could even imagine. Her grandmother and mother prayed and covered her life. Itchy's mother's prayer was fulfilled with her girls, and Itchy had to keep living to tell her story because her mother's struggle and the story were untold. She was raised in a blended family. Her mother remarried when she was six to her stepfather (Poppa), he had four daughters and her mother had four daughters. All her girls had a personal relationship with God, living well, educated, and married or had been married and divorced. Itchy and her oldest sister were divorced, and her other six sisters of seven were still married. They all attended college and received certifications, license, degrees, doctorates, and honors. Itchy's oldest sister Roxy, possess a realist mind set, introvert with frugal tendencies that loves her immediate family, she was also a caregiver to her mother, that lost her battle to Alzheimer. Annette is an Agent of Christ and nurturing kind soul and the matriarch with love of family. Brenda, a brilliant beautician with creative style in decorating and crafts has a great love for family and was a caregiver to several family members. Yolanda, a prayer warrior, with a yoke anointed to break the spirit of oppression in past life experiences. Willing to give her last. She also has the strength of ten thousand women, humble, and had a voice (sing) that demands your attention. Lillie who passed December of 2006 after fighting he battle with cancer was loving, encouraging listener and naturally creative love for family and kept the family at peace. Angela an Angel that loves God, her family, singing in the choir, with legs and beauty like a model, humble demeanor and good with numbers. Her and Itchy grew up sharing a bedroom.

Her sister, closest to her in age, Jacquelyn, is jubilant, judicious, and studious consistently educating herself and received her highest degree of a doctorate. She had received enough degrees to share with all of her sisters. She has a good sense of judgment, and concern for others and sacrifices her time and herself. She traveled the world speaking about medications that help people diagnosed with bipolar, manic depression, and Alzheimer's. In 2005, she volunteered to do missionary work in Uganda during her two-week vacation from Pfizer. They treated and gave out free medications for various infectious diseases from Malaria to HIV-related infections.

The little girl had lived so long crying out for help, looking for love, being insecure, and feeling others saw her as ugly. Itchy had to live to tell how she was victorious through God's grace! She was no longer afraid to take her mask off. Itchy began living life abundantly with transparency because God had manifested joy and happiness into her life that she longed for; 'at last' (song by Etta James), her love had finally come along, love of self.

CHAPTER NINE

Happy with Four Good Days

I T IS **2009,** and things are so much clearer now. When the United States voted its first Black President **Barack Obama,** into office. The song was **"Turning Me On"** by Keri Hilson, featuring T-Pain & Lil Wayne. In January, our family leased a 54-seat passenger bus to go to the inauguration, and we were there with millions of people. They met and dined at the well-known Wolfgang Puck restaurant and walked over twenty miles that day. It was a treat to see our own Aretha Franklin from Detroit sing and Beyoncé singing while crying 'At Last'. Another memorable moment. A historical step for African Americans; we had gone from a race being recognized as Negro, to Black to an African American being in the White House, what an accomplishment! Martin Luther King Jr. I have a dream speech came alive, and it didn't matter how many times we changed our name as a race; President Obama was elected for Change. For all those who fought for our rights and freedoms, this was a true beginning to show that America is a melting pot, and you can have equal opportunities. Enlightened that our

Black Ancestors in 1619 adapted to change by becoming Americans from Africa. Learning the American culture, how to farm, plow, blacksmith, carpenter, inventors, and most of all overcomers. At this point in life, it is clear she is still standing today because of God!

This was the same year attending the Murray Wright All Class Reunion at Bert's Place for the first time. Itchy ran into the Twin's from the class of 1982, grew up in Research Apartments, and Calvin who also attended Oakland University from the class of 1985. The event was nice, and Itchy Mae & her Sands attended for about two hours, and after leaving, they ended up on three flat tires, and that story nearly took them back twenty years, and they look back on it now and throw their heads back, holler laughing.

This was also the year being introduced to social network site Facebook and joined this site because her teenage daughter had a page, and Itchy wanted to monitor her. On the first day on the site, the first person's name was her high school male friend who went to the Army. At the time Booney was the one that helped to set up my page on Facebook and warned to be careful.

In April of 2009, they exchanged numbers over Facebook and was in contact; a few months later in May Itchy visited him in Texas, and he visited Michigan in August.

They became business partners, and it was obvious they were closer than most. Of course, Itchy Mae desired something more than he was ready for and was caught between love and lust. Knowing that Itchy was too old to get caught up in a fairy tale; it was time to get out of La-La Land and be realistic. It was clear not to mix business with pleasure because it can ruin a friendship. Itchy realized in that situation that her boots were made for walking and walking, in the other direction is what she did!

Now it is the end of 2009 and getting a friend request from another high school male friend that asked her to the prom in his senior year, and she was a freshman. The protection was having a strict mother and she would not allow me to go. Once again, thinking this man was the one! They went to the Murray Wright All Class Reunion on January 2, 2010, and later fell in love. They had so much in common and would travel from Detroit to Lansing every week to see each other. They both loved God and family, dancing, talking, exercising, and the same types of music. This relationship ended, and again gained five sisters (his oldest sister and two sets of twins), and out of the five, there was one sister that became very close, and they all are still in touch until this very day. Itchy then decided she had enough of social network relationships, and her outlook is she rather have loved and lost than never love at all! With the help of prayer to God to manifest happiness in her life, learned to become happily single and just sincerely happy (Humble, Ambitious, Prayerful, Passionate, and Yielding).

The Note from Facebook

I may know about exercising and nutrition and can write a nutrition plan and tell you how to speed up your metabolism. Now when it comes to relationships it's another story. Now I know a lot of you will probably say no she's not putting herself out there like that and talking about her personal business. My girls and my sisters are going to dethrone me from being the Queen that I am. Lol, well one thing I've learned in life is that a quiet mouth doesn't get fed and people are going to talk about you regardless of when you're doing good or bad. When you tell your business or try to keep it a secret. Plus, I don't fear man I Fear God. We must obey God as ruler rather than men. Acts 5:29.

As a single mother raising a teenage daughter and trying to be a positive role model and a Christian, you must keep your house in order and do things in decency and in order. I said that to say this, a Man is a Hero for having many relationships and a Woman is a Zero. There are talk shows, reality shows, and books (Steve Harvey Act Like a Woman & Think like Man) on relationships and getting married. The reality shows are over the top and it makes you think are they serious, desperate, or just broke and need the money? Did anybody want Flavor Flav? Any Body? At the end of the day, we were created by God who is love, and that is why we love.

Begin my story of relationships it starts a little something like this when I was a young adult I thought if a guy treats me nice and respected me, I was doing good. Then in my early twenties, I was in a relationship for 2 years and he asked me to marry him, so I did and stayed married for 13 years. Now being divorced for six years I have been in 3 relationships. Now understand me clearly relationships we are not talking about dates to dinner or the movies or dates every time a young man gives you flowers you have relations like the grandma in Nutty Professor. The first one was two years after my divorce and the second one the man just wanted to keep me on layaway and take me around as a showpiece and I wasn't tolerating that!! The third one was a committed relationship. Now saying that I must say I refuse to male bash because it's wrong and sisters we know we love our brothers. Please stop the male-bashing because it is contradictory, we usually stay with him or get back with him most of the time. It also makes it harder for the sister to come after you. Lol, then we get all the baggage and overflow from the man's prior relationships. Yes, men also have baggage as women do. Just as they gossip as women do. By the way drama also and Drama is something I don't do! You won't see me parking lot pimping, slashing tires, or busting the windows out the car.

I don't care how people say they won't let a prior relationship affect the current one we do carry hang-ups or tendencies into the new relationship. That is why it is good to take your time and do you and not rush right into another relationship.

In two of the instances, I chose the men because you know I'm very confident and think I have 'Game' LOL so to say I'm not with either of them today, so much for

Game. A loving relationship is not full of games, tricks, and conditions!! Finally, I said I'm going to wait on the Lord, and there he was.......... He chose me and found me...

Mr. Right? God Sent?? You could not keep us apart and we both thought what we had was so Divine!! We planned to get married and just live happily ever after and then it ended. BOOM!! The honeymoon stage was over as they call it, even though the marriage vows were never exchanged. Was it Lust, Love, or Infatuation? The Bible says, in Jeremiah 17: 9 the heart is more treacherous than anything else and is desperate. Who can know it? Timing is everything it can mean a 'World' of a difference.

I don't believe in making New Year's Resolutions as I shared with you all in January. I said the first 6 months I was going to mind my own business and for the last 6 months I was going to stay out of other people's business and throughout the year, I was going to make people smile. Well, I know a lot of you all are smiling and laughing to see this woman talking about her business. For those of you that don't get it, yet my business is a service to females from ages 8 to 80 about your nutritional, physical, and mental health. I have workshops to help empower women with their self-esteem, and self-confidence, improve sisterhood, and stop repeating cycles (family curses) of abuse, molestation, and abandonment. Therefore, if I can't be real and discuss a common issue amongst my sisters about relationships and marriage, and not act like I'm 'Brand New 'while the media discuss it all the time. Oh Well!!

One of my little sisters from my extended family whom I lived across the street from for 13 years said my status after my relationship status changed to single. Is there something in the water? My reply was NO, it's called Life. My sister and I have a saying and we throw our heads back while laughing and say, Ride Baby Ride. Life is likened to a roller coaster you wait in line for hours to experience the speed and the adrenaline rush while you scream and HOLD on, while the ride only last seconds or minutes. In Life, things may happen to us for weeks, months, or years until we no longer decide to HOLD on. Let it Go and Let God!! As bad as we may not want to admit it, we allow things to happen to us in life far too long that we have the control to end the ride in minutes. I believe that we all just want to be happy and have a companion we can relate to and grow old with. I don't believe people grow apart. I believe we change as we get older and want different things, will no longer accept certain things, get tired of the dumb stuff, and decide we're getting too old to sweat the small stuff. Then it's some people that compromise and have all the same feelings as the people above but decide to make it work no matter what the underlined issues are. I told my sister the other day that it is easy to be Selfish and hard work is Selfless.

I believe when you decide to have a 'Real' relationship it is no longer all about yourself it's about the other person. That is a very tall order to fill. Many may say that you are supposed to love yourself first and not lose yourself in the other person and your identity and that is true!! The funny thing I have noticed is all the wonderful couples that are still making it work have learned to balance those things. That is something I'm lacking in Balance. One of my sisters told me not to become anyone's Everything!! You cannot be a person everything takes away from your self-esteem and your power to survive and it is unrealistic!!! We are all imperfect beings and only Jesus Christ should be put on a pedestal as your EVERYTHING!!

Some may call me crazy when I'm just a simple Romantic. I love music and the message it provides it can truly be therapy to your soul. I have listened to songs like "Dangerously in Love" by Beyoncé, 'Almost Doesn't Count by Brandy, 'Deuces' by Chris Brown, 'I hope she cheats on you by Marsha Ambrosius, 'You made a fool of me' by Meshell Ndegeocello, 'Blame it on me by Chrisette Michele. "Slow Down" by Indie Arie is something that my Mommy tells me, 'Healing for my Soul' by Kelly Price, and 'Gotta Get my Heart Back', by Keyshia Cole.

Not until a week ago did, I finally begin to laugh when I listen to 'Lovesick' by Priscilla Renea and thought it was too cute and it applied to the situation. Through all of this, I have learned another life lesson and I will continue to love, laugh, and wait on the Lord.

Isn't it funny how you can be in the hustle and bustle of things in your life, and you're not going anywhere? All the noise can distract you from hearing from God, while you are working on yourself. Itchy heard people all around her talking but saying nothing. It was not until Itchy listened to this voice that wasn't extremely loud or soft-spoken that she realized it was time to yield and pay attention. No, she wasn't hallucinating or losing her mind! Some may call it your conscience, and others say it was God talking. Remember the scene in the movie Color Purple where the choir sang God is trying to tell you something right now? That is precisely how Itchy felt. She STOPPED everything to listen because she didn't want to miss out on valuable information. Some people don't believe in miracles today, but Itchy can tell you that she was next in line for her Miracle to happen, and you couldn't tell her it wasn't!

Through all Itchy trials, she never left God and knew he carried her throughout her entire forty-four years. Her relationship with God only grew closer and more vital. Itchy fought with depression and suicidal thoughts most of her life and finally remembered someone telling her that many great and even brilliant people have a deficiency and realized that she turned a harmful disorder into positive energy. Itchy never thought of herself as intelligent, so this never meant much to her the same way she never thought she was beautiful.

Itchy Mae was excellent in discerning the beauty, strength, and elegance in other women in the family and women in the movies, music, and poetry industries. Always admired actresses such as Lena Horne, Angela Bassett, Loretta Divine, Halle Berry, Nia Long, Malinda Williams & Kerry Washington. Admired Chante Moore, Tamia, Yolanda Adams, Beyoncé, Chrisette Michelle & Ledisi in the music industry. When it comes to phenomenal poets, Maya Angelou & Nikki Giovanni are profound. Then, a couple of sultry singers also put their poetry to music, like Lauryn Hill, Jill Scott & India Arie. A few Black women of elegance, Diane Carol, Diana Ross, & Michelle Obama. They were all my sisters in my head. The phrase that best describes my thought process in most recent years, quoting Marianne Williamson, "Our deepest fear is not that we are inadequate. Our deepest fear is that we are powerful beyond measure. We ask ourselves, who am I to be brilliant, gorgeous, talented, and fabulous? Actually, who are you not to be? We were born to make manifest the glory of God that is within us. And we let our light shine, and we unconsciously give other people permission to do the same."

There may have been dying all around from a tender young age, but there was a lot of living going on! Itchy Mae dealt with depression throughout the years, and it takes a lot of discipline and prayer not to depend on medication and choose LIFE! This is not a recommendation to only seek therapy, some individuals may require taking medication based on the diagnosis. Itchy is sharing how she handled things. Remember one thing for certain is life will keep going <u>with</u> or <u>without</u> you. Don't get stuck or over think things.

The intent is for women worldwide to laugh, love, and live because you only get four good days. The four good days theory goes something like this, there are four Sundays in most months, a day of rest that's the first outlook. Then the other perspective is most females are on their menstrual cycle for 3 to 7 days and off 23 to 27 days, leaving four days. During the days you're off your cycle, you ovulate, and after you ovulate, you have mood swings, and PMS, and then you're back on your cycle again, and for those over 40, you may begin going into perimenopause.

On any given day you may find me writing short stories and poems. Itchy Mae love volunteering at Covenant House Michigan, working out with groups of women, or just having coffee and conversation at a local library with a group of women that is helping to restore their joy in life.

This book is also dedicated to women that have struggle with depression, abusive relationships, being a mother, a wife, working, and raising a family while completing a degree. Two things we can't avoid are our menstrual cycles and menopause, and at the end of the day, there are only four good days out of a month, so make the best of them!

WHO AM I?

I am more than what lies beneath this skin
I have touched many hearts from deep within
I am more than your eyes can see
I am a woman that proclaims victory
I am more than my hips and thighs
That blows so many men's minds
I am not a Shero or Superwoman at any time
I am a virtuous woman and don't feel confined
I am a Queen for those that wonder why
It is because my Father said, "I am" countless times
My Father is the King of kings that
created this entire world
I inherited more than wealth and beautiful pearls
He has erased all my guilt and shame
I am a Queen an original design with dignity
It is because my Father said, "I am"
and that is the reason why

Author: Joi C. Spencer

MY SISTERS KEEPER

When my sister walks with her head
down low it is for me..............

To tell my sister to keep your head up
and this too shall pass one day.

When my sister current situation don't
seem promising it is for me

To tell my sister don't let your problem
control you, control your problem.

When my sister yells out profane
language it is for me....

To tell my sisters watch your SPEECH because
there is death and life in your TONGUE.

When my sister talks negative about
another sister it is for me

To tell my sister this is the time to build up
and to stop tearing one another down.

When my sister thinks her life circumstances
or accomplishments are more important
than the next sisters it is for me.

To tell my sister that we all are UNIQUE and have our own stories and deserve to be heard and RESPECTED!

When my sister gets overconfident and
forgets that she once travel the same road
that many are still on it is for me.

To tell my sister stay humble and don't be so quick
to forget your past and the people you have passed
by, that help you to reach this point of success.

When my younger sisters ask what inheritance
has, she been left I can tell them.

Young sister you were left the Legacy of wealth
of knowledge, wisdom, love, and respect
you are a young Queen in training!!

Author: Joi C. Spencer

CHAPTER TEN

Universal Precautions

IN SOCIETY, MOST people sum each other up through observation. In most cases, relationships begin through observing the way another person acts. When men choose females, they tend to scope out each option first before picking their prey. A perfect example is the club setting, and while men already know their mission, they watch the female activity. Some females may have come to party with their friends for fun, while others are trying to get chosen. Men recognize the signs and plan appropriately. The men plan to identify the difference in the women and approach them on that basis. As women, we must switch to a male's approach by listening and watching. Some of the observations about men is never to give out too much information so that the man can become who you want him to become temporarily.

Women must be selfish regarding ourselves, our children, and our homes. It is not acceptable to let your children meet every man you date. There is no problem with going to the movies or out to eat with someone. However, just because it was considered a date for you does not mean it is an introduction for your children. As women, we are supposed to treat ourselves as royalty.

Ordinary people are not always allowed past the gates. Holding yourself to this higher standard sets a guideline and boundaries in a man's eyes.

Today, this is required. Just as your children are treated as special air looms, you should treat your home just the same.

Nowadays, women are quick to hand out a key to their home, but this is the biggest mistake.

Once you open your home, you are now opening your place of peace. The home is the palace of your royal status. Men will take advantage of most opportunities; they only do what we allow as women. You must consider if the person would make an extra key or even begin moving into your home without permission. Be aware that most of these decisions are made because of clouded judgment, which soon misleads your beliefs about the male persona.

Some women go to the club to have a good time, and others go to meet men. When you are introduced to a man, this is not the time to let your guard down. Itchy was introduced her

ex-husband through a coworker. It was assumed that this was a safer alternative than meeting someone at a club. However, this would not make much of a difference after time goes on.

In my early twenties there was a time span of being in and out of short-term relationships ranging from six to eight months and began to think it was time to settle down in a committed relationship that would lead to marriage. When her Coworker mentioned introducing her to his cousin, she thought no at first and later decided to go out to a restaurant a few months later. The first date was nice at Chi Chi's in Dearborn, Michigan, and then afterward, they hung out at known Bar & Grill Downtown. While at St Antoine Bar & Grill warning signs were coming left and right. Well-dressed men of a particular status, wearing Dobbs and Furs would approach our table. Sometimes men will not lie they decide to omit information if you don't ask. While sitting at the small table along the side of the wall near the bar looking puzzled. No poker face from this woman. Then man asked are you okay? Then Itchy responded, how do you know all these men. That's when he confessed that he was back from vacation visiting a county facility in Ohio for six months. The charges were for being an unlicensed pharmacist. The weird thing is after their first date they were together all the time, and six months into the relationship, he asked her to marry him. The plot thickens and the control begins as concern and love.

Things were moving so fast, that she moved into River Place Apartments in February, and by April, he asked to move in. There was no way she would live with him, and he knew this, so that is when he asked to marry her and planned to get married the following year in 1991. Shortly after he moved in, the signs began to show, and Itchy was in denial. When a person reveals who they are, believe them and take note. A little history on 500 River Place, 4 stories apartment community was built in 1908 as a warehouse and remodeled in 1985 with townhouse and completed by 1989. Later in 1991 penthouses were added over the parking garage.

It is six months after living together, and the control, drinking, and physical abuse happen. Itchy Mae was shocked, hurt, and more embarrassed than anything to tell anyone. What was my family and friends going to think? There was no way her mom or sisters would allow her to marry him after he hit her, so she kept it a secret and married him anyway. She was not afraid of him, and was more so concerned because he played on my emotions. Thinking she was going to help him fix his anger problems. He would say no one believed in him, and stories that his mother abandoned him at a young age. Lastly, he would ask, are you going to leave me too? This was part of the manipulation and control that many abusers operate in.

The control fits of anger, arguments followed by profane language and degrading remarks, and threats of leaving began. The constant reinforcement of the words to love bomb you started,

'I love you, and I didn't mean that, or I didn't mean to put you down. The verbal abuse had become a regular thing. At this particular time, Itchy was not dependent on this man. In a good a space, confident, college-educated, working full time in the Banking Industry for about five years, leasing my first apartment, and buying a car, a red 1989 Chevrolet Beretta.

This lesson taught me about taking people for face value and not believing every word they say, especially when it comes from a man that said, he loves you. The Bible also speaks about this in Proverbs 14:15, anyone inexperienced puts faith in every word, but the shrewd one considers his steps.

The year is **2010,** and there is much wisdom gained through relationships with men and friendships with women. Women, if you are the type to think with your eyes and heart and not with your mind or gut feelings, you need to use universal precautions. There will always be a man who seems like he is the nicest guy, and this rule wouldn't apply; WRONG!

This is also the year the Detroit Red Wings won the most Stanley Cups (11) Championships than any NHL franchise, and the Detroit Lions were one of the four NFL teams that had not gone to the Super Bowl. And the year that I had the opportunity to meet the famous boxer Milton McCrory a former WBC World Welterweight champion that fought out of the legendary *Kronk Gym* in Detroit, Michigan. Milton McCrory attended Pershing High School's All Class Reunion at the Keynote Lounge.

Also, the year Steve Harvey's book on relationships was released, which I have plans to read it during one of those four good days. Now Itchy's friend Yvonne told her never to forget that dating is liken to a 'Party.' That is saying to know your place as a woman; for instance, when you go to a party, some women are looking to network, drink, a relationship, have sex, or dance.

The men plan to identify the difference in the women and approach them on that basis.

The' Party' means to have fun, know when to leave, stick to your plan and don't switch to his agenda. Some of the things Itchy learned about men is never to give out too much information, so that man can become who you want him to become temporarily. For instance, if you want to drink Cîroc and party like a rock star, he is your Puff Daddy. Then if you want to dance provocatively, he's your Usher, making love up in the club. Watch out if you share you want to get married; he speeds the relationship up with words you want to hear that are not put into action.

Next, never hand out any keys because you will never get your control back or your freedom, and even if the key is given back, change the locks in case the person already made a spare key. Next, never go into a relationship with a man that just ended a relationship to start a new relationship with you. Take it from me the same way you got him will be the same way you lose him. Karma is something else because sometimes it will come back on you when you least expect it! Itchy knew that the two men she loved dearly ended a relationship and started one with her and then started a new relationship before ending theirs. The first instance was her

ex-husband claiming, he ended a long-term relationship before they started dating, and the young woman ended up being a fatal attraction, almost costing both of them their lives. The second instance was the most recent relationship. The guy ended a relationship a week after starting a relationship with Itchy, and she told him she could wait until he was clear on his decision. Instead, she walked right into the trap again, thinking with my heart.

Love and relationships can get tricky but go with your gut feeling. Another hint is to give yourself time to finish your unfinished business before pulling another person into the mix. In some instances, it has cost some innocent people their lives. For relationships that involve children, never talk negatively about the child's father around the child because you are only hurting yourself. Don't lie either but talk about their good qualities. When a child constantly hears negative things being said, they either despise the parent who talks about the other parent or loses respect for the other parent. As women, we wonder why so many men wonder if their mother loved them or was proud of them. For most of their lives, they heard this, no good this, and no good that. Then, the young girls believe that most men are dogs and no good. They start to say things like I'm not going to take that when I grow up, or I'm not getting married. Generations of women break the fundamentals of family life and having both parents in the household. Being independent is overrated when comes to raising a family. Women need to wake up! Just because we can become independent don't make it right and a village is needed to raise African American children.

For women dating, do not introduce your child to the men you date. You may go to dinner and a movie that is not a reason to introduce your child to them. Your child should be treated like a precious, priceless air loom, and you wouldn't trust a stranger with your precious air loom or leave them alone with your valuables. Having an imagination as an adult can work in your favor. Itchy would tell my daughter that she is the Princess in training, and she was the Queen and their house was their castle. Why would common folk or strangers need to enter their Castle or domain? One's home is private, and where you go for peace and peace of mind is priceless. Until this day my daughter mentions that I did not let a lot of people come to visit.

Another thing women are encouraged to do is establish a friend that you can tell when you're going on a date without putting that pressure on their young or teenage children. Yes, it is okay to meet people at a restaurant, movie, or concert until you get to know them! Your safety is essential but not your children's responsibility. The time to introduce the man is once you the pair of you establish your status as an acquaintance, friend, or a serious relationship past six months. It maybe old fashion to ask a man what Am I to you. Survey say's if you have to ask you may qualify as a friend. Women, there is a difference; the habit of making someone your Boo or man before you know all the qualifiers. Never assume! Follow your gut feeling when you see boundaries being crossed, confront them head-on, and if it happens again, dismiss the relationship.

Another thing learned is that men will tell you everything you need to know and will only do what a woman allows them to do. Sometimes we are so busy giggling, talking and not listening. Listening is a skill, let the person finish talking and not interrupt them before their complete thought is stated. People usually pause when they want you to respond.

For example, if he tells you he's been told in previous relationships of being controlling, he is. Another example is if he tells you he was a womanizer, he's not fully recovered. An example of crossing your boundaries is if you tell a man that you don't introduce your child to men you date, and he persists in taking you all to dinner or comes over before calling, he is testing boundaries. You can do one or two things by not answering the door or not going to dinner. I guarantee you that if you don't answer the door, he will be angry, but you will still have your foundation in place with your child's safety. He will call you and bring it up, and that is your opportunity to address it. Don't go soft now; you need to speak your mind without being rude but speak boldly about how you notice he can't respect your wishes and then ask why he thinks he should meet your child after such a short time. A wise man will not only respect you more, and he will understand and continue dating you, or he will keep it moving.

Now for family, please don't introduce everyone to that man, and then in three months, you're introducing another man. That is tacky and not coifed! Some women give men too much power, and men don't have to earn anything these days. Traditionally men had to date you and climb to the top of the tree to earn meeting your child, family, and even having sex with you. Many women want to know where the respect went and say shivery is dead. We can't blame the men for getting use to a certain response. It's not the men's fault; it's our fault, ladies. The man didn't change; the woman has changed, and many have lost their Queen status that they so quickly gave away! A man that intends on being around can wait and will wait. Yes, men can act like animals, mark their territory, and have their eyes set on their prey, and they will do whatever it takes to get you.

They will stay focused on their prey (the woman) for a specific duration. Just keep in mind that some men wait, and once they conquer you sexually, they are gone. Then some men will wait, and once they conquer you sexually, they control or own you now. Then some men wait because they are tired of the games themselves and not in a rush to go anywhere fast, so successful women are strategic and know what they want and the difference between the three types of men.

Women, we can learn from our own mistakes and learn to date a man the way we would want a young man to date our daughter. In other words, we give out a lot of good advice; now it's time to follow it. Women, mark their territory as well by purposely leaving items at the home. It is one thing to leave things when you have discussed them and another to leave things when you're fishing for information your gut feeling has already told you.

As Tyler Perry's famous stage play Class Reunion addressed, when you think your man is cheating, he is. Don't start anything you don't want to be done to you. You may begin to play- house, and then it's the handing out the keys issue. It's called 'Trust" it is nothing wrong with two adults having their own place, especially when children are involved. Marking your territory can backfire on you or explode in your face. Women have shared stories that they left an earring and next time the man visits her home he brings it and a few outfits to leave at her place. Next time he brings more cloth's until he suggest they should move in together. When you don't agree on moving in together the check in regularly throughout the day starts and one thing leads to another, and the next thing, you begin feeling like you have a GPS or low jack on your body.

Last but not least, have enough sense to know if you haven't seen your ex in several months, and then he wants to drop some things off to you that you left at his home, and he wants to return them late in the evening. Please recognize this is a 'Bootie Call' and don't beg or belittle yourself decline the visit. Doing this keeps your dignity because a 'Lady' knows not to hate the 'Player' just don't become part of his 'Game.'

Now for friendship with women, it's simple, if you can count your friends on more than one hand, you're in denial and have a Pink Elephant in the room. Some women will only become friends with men because they say they can't trust women or are jealous of them they're in denial over an issue that several women have confronted them with. This female gets into a lot of drama, has a lot of mouth, and doesn't know when to stop or frequent places that she thinks just because someone talks to her that they're her girl. She has flirted, dated, or slept with her so-called friend's man. Then there are the women that make every other female they meet their friend; they too are in denial. A true friend is someone male or female that respects you. They can tell you the truth, and they don't judge you, know your most embarrassing moment, know you, know your family, give you their last, and will not let you keep living your life with a Pink Elephant in the room.

In closing, for clarification the intentions are not to say ALL men have an agenda or are up to no good. Neither is the attempt to male bash men because there are women that have the same characteristics with agendas of their own. That would be considered stereotyping and judgmental. It goes without saying to acknowledge good men that can fill the shoes that are very hard to walk in during this day and age and hold down the role of being a 'Good Man.' This is Itchy Mae story and things she observed while being single, married and divorced, and dating again, so please apply when necessary.

Itchy lost her mother's father and godfather in **1972, her** dad's father in **1988**, and her stepfather in **2003** from Lung Cancer. Itchy godmother died in **2001** from complications after having a triple bypass surgery at the age of eighty-seven, and Itchy had one sister that died from Cancer in **2006** at the age of fifty-one. Both Itchy's grandmothers had longevity. Itchy mom's mother died in **2002** at the age of ninety-one from Alzheimer's, her dad's mother died in **2007** from natural causes at the age of One hundred one, and her daddy in **2016** from congested heart failure. Itchy's mother is alive now ninety-one. Her loving father made his transition on April 14, **2016**, at eighty-four.

Over five decades of Itchy's life, she has put a swing in her hip, a slide in her glide, with a smile. All Thanks to

God for all his grace! Itchy thought there was nothing so wrong that a piece of sweet chewing gum couldn't solve it. Itchy likes the scene from the movie 'Kingdom Come' when Toni Braxton plays the role of the rich man's wife. Itchy must live to talk about the Kingdom of God that the Bible speaks about and tell the legacy of the phenomenal women in the family to her daughter, seven nieces, five nephews, twelve great-nieces, and three great-nephews, and three great- great nieces.

CHAPTER ELEVEN

Exposing The Enemy – From A Mother's Point of View

T HE IRONY OF the entire story is that my life was like a nightmare that you never wake up from, and no one explained anything to me. Many people have talents they know they are good at, and others don't realize their talents. As for Itchy Mae she, knew early on her talent was helping others, nurturing, and finding the good in all people. My acquired talent has caused me much grief, drained me mentally, and developed my patience. Itchy eventually learned not to pray for patience; because when God gives you a way out, take it. The information being shared is research done over the last 32 years is not scientific studies or statistics; it all comes from wisdom, observation, and experience. Itchy observed how her dad had an episode every fifteen years in 1983, 1998, & 2013 after he stopped taking his medication or the medication was decreased.

Many people say, "you must be crazy" or "out of your mind." In general, this applies to the day-to-day life of many people that suffer from depression or bipolar disorder. Believe it or not, many people are functioning with bipolar and have never been diagnosed, just like there are functioning alcoholics. The first time hearing the term bipolar used was in 1983. My father had a nervous breakdown after not taking his medication and was admitted to Walter Ruther Mental Facility in Northville. My dad stopped taking his medication and had a bipolar/schizophrenic episode involving hallucinating: people attacking him, bugs were on him, and hearing voices. As a teenager, you don't understand any of this. Itchy Mae had never lived in the same household with her dad to see the signs, so when he didn't make it to her graduation, Itchy just figured he was sick in the hospital until her oldest sister took her to visit him in Northville. Daddy was so happy to see the both of us, and Itchy was elated to see her daddy. At this particular time, she still did not understand his sickness.

Later in 1998, my dad had another episode after his psychiatrist lowered the dose of his medication. He had been on the same medication for over 40 years, his doctor fearing it was affecting his heart. This was when the *enemy* exposed himself. Detroit police and EMS were called to take him to Holy Cross Hospital, and he was admitted for three weeks. Eventually, the family had to decide rather we should admit him back to the Northville facility.

Itchy's dad had previously shared some horror stories, explaining how they treated him at the facility. Usually, the methods used were injecting him with medicine to calm him or applying electric shock. We then decided not to admit him, which was the best thing we could have done. Now at this time, Itchy daughter was two years old, and her and her dad had become closer than ever before. There was only one problem. Itchy had been married for about seven years, in an abusive marriage unbeknownst to her dad.

As we hear many times, it is a small world. One experience was when my stepbrother visited our neighbor downstairs when we lived in a two-family flat. Soon came to find out that he told my dad he heard us fighting upstairs. Before getting married, my husband's mother told me he had nervous energy and was hyperactive; needless to say, Itchy did not know what that meant. It later became apparent when he would either sleep for long periods or have sleepless nights, which resulted in drinking, smoking, gambling, making risky decisions, and starting fights over anything. Itchy husband told her that she was crazy and needed to seek help for a chemical imbalance. Being the loving and doting wife she was, she went to a therapist, and she evaluated me and shared that nothing was wrong with me. She included that just my dad was diagnosed with bipolar, but it did not mean she was bipolar.

Furthermore, she shared that my husband was long-term depressive, bipolar, and narcissistic. Itchy was floored and glad to finally have someone explain why he acted the way he did. It was the behavior she hated, not him, so she agreed to help him and encourage him to take medicine. But he would take medicine for about a week. Then one day, while driving down the street, he threw the pills out the window. His reasoning was they made him zombie-like and decreased his sex drive. The fighting continued to fast-forward six months, so Itchy moved out and filed for divorce a second time. Once Itchy returned a year later, the fighting had stopped, but things were complicated, and by then, she was tired and filed for the third and final divorce. Itchy Mae refused to raise her daughter to live under dysfunctional conditions and soon assume that was natural behavior between a husband and wife. Our daughter was eight years old, and she saw enough trauma twice, too many times. Some may debate that ending the marriage, changed her daily routine of seeing her father is now a broken home to become a single mom. In reality you do a child and yourself more harm to remain in an abusive marriage. Keep in mind you constantly are trying to hide the truth and end up lying to your child/children. It effects that child for life! They eventually agreed to put their differences aside and co-parent our daughter.

After that, Itchy thought it would be a good idea for my daughter and her father to continue seeking counseling and therapy from the same clinic that diagnosed her father. You know the saying "a parent knows their child," and noticed similar behaviors with their daughter being hyper like her father. They had a very high IQ, would get bored quickly, and lacked confidence. The therapist said she was an average developing child at that particular time. Then by the age of eleven, she was doing great in school as usual and usually played dual sports each year, such as karate, cheerleading, basketball, volleyball, and track. Later through the years, she was going through puberty, and Itchy noticed a few things that concerned her, but she did not want to be in denial. It seemed like she had to constantly keep her busy to keep her focused and control behavior issues. In addition, Itchy could not distinguish if she was going through usual adolescent problems or was the behavior related to a mental disorder. However, she did excellent in her academics, GPA of 3.7- 4.0, and even in high school. Soon my daughter figured that her grades would overshadow the behaviors. She was inducted into the Honor Society & Great Lakes Scholars. We moved and I changed her school once again. Itchy questioned if she had made the right decision to change her school so many times. They moved to keep her near her job and due to getting calls from the school about her behavior.

Now the year is 2010, we had just returned from my niece's sixteenth birthday party, and to my surprise, Itchy entered the bathroom to find out that her daughter was a cutter. She slammed and locked the door, forcing her to pull the door off the hinges to get to her to remove the knife. Then she pointed the knife at her, and Itchy yelled, "Are you crazy? We don't do things like suicide."

Itchy immediately called her therapist, and she told her to take her to an emergency so they could admit her to the hospital for treatment. Itchy didn't listen, only thinking, "Not my child." Day one of denial was the Fourth of July weekend. Itchy woke her up the following day, and we went to Lansing for a Holiday party. While there, she didn't want to be around anyone or come out of the house. An example of Itchy's poor judgment by not addressing the issue and taking her to the hospital for observation. Later realizing she was crying out for help and didn't know where to start. Itchy began thinking about it; first, it was because her parents divorced when she was eight. Then Itchy asked her if someone had violated her. She figured something traumatic in her life was causing this behavior. Itchy never thought it could be that *enemy* lurking called bipolar. Shortly after, we stopped going to therapy, and both parents tried doing more with her and paying closer attention.

One year later, in 2011, all hell broke loose, and the *Enemy* appeared again. Our daughter was attending Farmington High School and returning to school in September for her sophomore year, and in October, the calls began coming in about behavior issues. The school principal, assistant principal, and school social worker were all in my corner, trying to help us. Itchy would ask her to tell me the truth, so she would not be embarrassed when talking to the school administrators. Our daughter would lie to me, and they would tell us they had it on video or that another teacher witnessed her actions. Not until she was in a fight defending herself was, she suspended from school for the first time. After her behavior worsened, the school social worker referred me to New Oakland Adolescent Center and Oakland County Incorrigible process to fill out documents.

The last straw was when Itchy received a call from Farmington Hills Police that her daughter was detained for stealing an Arizona iced tea out of the Mobil gas station on Drake & Grand River. Come to find out, the Officer stated he knew she had fifty dollars in her purse. Itchy left work to pick her up from the police station, asking her, "What do you have to say about your behavior? Why would you steal when you had money?" Her response was surprising, "If that were my child, I would have left her at the police station to learn a lesson." After that response, Itchy took her home to write a letter to take back up to the Mobil station to apologize and to ask if she could volunteer to clean up. The gas attendant told me that her peers encouraged her behavior. My daughter would frequent that store by herself and never stole anything; however, her group was on video stealing.

Two different Farmington Police Officers would voluntarily come by the house to talk to my daughter to encourage her to do the right thing. They shared how they knew she was a good student from talking to the administrators at her school and that she had a mother that cared. After that incident, Itchy scheduled her first appointment at New Oakland Adolescent Center for a consultation with a psychiatrist. The psychiatrist was informative. He diagnosed her with bipolar and explained everything thoroughly. She was in a manic state at the time, making impulsive and risky decisions. He weighed her and gave us a prescription for Abilify 1 mg, later increasing it to 5mg. He explained that studies were still being done on medications for teenagers with bipolar 1 and informed us the studies were incomplete. Now being African American a lot of people and parents are not willing to participate in the trials or studies, so it is difficult to determine the right dosage.

Later in 2012, Itchy had just self-published her first short story, "Itchy Mae as the Human butterfly," and was having a book signing in January. My daughter attended the book signing, and she read the well-known poem "Our Deepest Fear" by Marianne Williamson. Itchy did not know if she should be excited or devastated because of what her and her daughter were facing. Itchy never wanted her daughter to be labeled as disabled, so she pushed her to her fullest potential and never gave up on her. The medication would make her zombie-like until it was in her system good enough. Her daughter had eighteen volunteer runaways that Itchy made police reports by the month of February. Fortunately, the cell phone provider, AT&T, had a tracking device that she could use to locate her until she realized it and deactivated it. She would sneak out the window or door while Itchy was asleep. An alarm sensor on the door would sound off; however, there was not a sensor on her bedroom window. She would sometimes sleep in the laundry room of our complex, in the clubhouse, or at her friend's house in our complex.

On one occasion she walked from Warren back to Farmington Hills. When she came home, she hadn't taken her medicine in days, and Itchy would journal her daughters behavior and her episodes occurring about every three weeks. Itchy eventually took her to Botsford, and after talking to the social worker at the hospital, they transferred her to Havenwyck in Auburn Hills, and she was admitted there for nine days. In March, she returned to school and was fine for about a week, and the behavior started again. Itchy would leave work on her lunch break to take her to therapy and then return to work. At this time, Itchy had not missed any days at work, so she applied for FMLA to cover her position. Soon after her Manager started to have another Team Member look for errors in her daily audits as an Auditor. The new manager at that time came in like a storm, terminating one of my co-workers the first month she managed our team. The manager had a problem with our team because she felt we were overpaid. She had plans to decrease our salaries to match her teams that we merged with ours at the beginning of the year.

Before my daughter's behavioral issues, Itchy maintain 96-100% on her Audit Reviews. Itchy received a warning, then a written letter about errors being made. In one meeting, she told them how they were overpaid and that none of us had degrees and didn't deserve the pay they were receiving. Itchy Mae spoke up and told her that she did have a Bachelor of Science in Business Management, and after that statement, she would say things like, "You think too much of yourself." The way Itchy was treated went from friendly inquiries to challenges. For Example: How well do you know how to use Excel? Are you familiar with Access? The Manager was always trying to appear she was part of the good ole boys club and wanted to fit in and was lackluster about anyone liking her or her macro managing style. She was not tactful and would discipline co-workers in front of everyone to the point they would cry, so Itchy went to HR to see how close they were to approving her FMLA and mentioning her unacceptable behavior. A week later, a meeting was called between Itchy and her Manager, and she denied it all. The team member that was disciplined nor any other team member would not inform HR of any of her taunting behavior.

In April, the following month, Itchy Mae gave her letter of resignation to begin care for her daughter full-time. Itchy filled out the paperwork for Makayla to become incorrigible by Oakland County, and she was placed in Children Village, Mandy's Place Emergency Shelter Care, and attending school there. She was released in May and returned to Farmington Hills High School. She was now on two medications, Abilify 10 mg, and Lamictal 25 mg. Abilify was for her depression, and Lamictal was a mood stabilizer to prevent manic and depressive episodes. Some of the side effects she experienced were tremors, dizziness, sweating, weight gain, and changes in the menstrual cycle. We also had to make sure that neither medicine affected her birth control pill. After returning to school, she would get weird stares and comments because part of being on the Oakland County program, she had to wear a tether to slow her from running away, and she was on probation for six months. If she missed a call or ran away, it was an automatic stay at Children Village Detention Facility. To graduate as scheduled, she had to attend summer school to take only two classes. After summer school was over in July, she began getting very defiant again, and the last of the last straw was when we were in a literal fistfight. As you may have heard, the strength of a bipolar person increases in a manic state. It took everything in me to restrain her and get her out of my house. Itchy immediately called the Farmington Hills Police, and they picked her up and took her over to my mother's house. That same day was the first day at my new job with a well-known Mortgage Company. Life happened again, and Itchy had to take control of the problem and not let the problem control her, so she went to her new job with a happy face.

The *enemy* appeared again, and she was placed in Children Village Detention Center from August 2012 until October 2012. Her dad disagreed with the process of the Oakland County incorrigible program, so he went to court to get her released into his care and moved her in with him and registered her at Fitzgerald High School in Warren. She was starting her junior year at a new school. She also stayed with her dad's parents due to him working afternoons. By this time, she had gained weight from the medications and didn't know anyone at school. She felt I didn't love her anymore and that she was overweight and depressed. This led her to take several pills while at her grandparent's home; this was her second suicide attempt. Her grandparents are the reason she is living today. They came back home after attending their meeting at the Kingdom Hall to find her lying on the bathroom floor unconscious, and they both began administering CPR and then called EMS. This was in the month December; the EMS took her to Children's Hospital. When Itchy got the call, her heart left my body, and my guilt slapped me in the face. Itchy called her family; her dad, stepmom, and her sister met her at Children's; she was admitted for seven days' then transferred to Henry Ford Kingswood, where she stayed for a month.

My dad had stopped taking his medicine and was admitted into Receiving Hospital in January 2013.

He stopped because he was devastated seeing his granddaughter suffering from the same disorder. He was thrown off schedule of taking his medicine as he would pray for hours, and he went into a manic-depressive state. During one of my visits to see my dad, he was not having a good day, and while in a manic phase, he told Itchy not to talk back to him, and she continued talking, so he slapped her clear across the room. She knew her dad was in there, so she looked in his eyes and asked him," So this is how you treat someone who loves you?" The incident broke her spirit for a while. Itchy called her mom crying. And she said, "don't go to visit him every day until the medicine stabilizes him," and we prayed. He was released from the hospital in mid-February 2013. We all praised God when he was stable and able to go home, and Itchy Mae had forgiven her dad. It's the behavior you dislike, not your loved one.

It wasn't easy when she returned to school. Her GPA dropped below 3.7 for the first time, down to 2.2. She told me that she was considering dropping out of school. A few weeks later, it was Parent Teachers Conference, and Itchy asked her daughter's dad to meet her at the school, and we agreed that we couldn't allow her to drop out.

Each teacher we sat down to talk with had great things to say about her. Itchy shared with each of them that she was thinking of dropping out. They all encouraged her to complete school; she only had one more year. There was one teacher who told our daughter that if she could raise her GPA to 2.5, she would make her a member of the Student Council. By the end of the school year in June, Makayla finished with a 2.8, although she missed a lot of school and did make-up work. It is Fall 2013 senior year. Makayla had lost weight due to being on the cheer team. In October, she was scheduled to take her senior pictures at her grandparent's house by an independent photographer. Then in December, she received her first report card marking and received a 4.0 GPA.

In 2014 she shared that she had not taken her meds and did not want to take them any longer. She had applied to four colleges, two in-state Western Michigan and Central Michigan, and two out-of-state colleges, Tennessee State University & North Carolina AT&T. We went to tour TSU in April. She was accepted, so we went home to plan for her move. We looked for dresses in February; it was approaching prom time, and everything was going well. It was time for Prom, and she had the red carpet, and limo and all the family went to her dad's house to see her to Prom. More excitingly, she won the best dress and free pictures. It was the end of the school year and report card time again, and she had a 4.0 GPA once again, an award for leadership and honor roll. I refuse to give up on my daughter or let her give up on herself. Itchy didn't let her diagnosis disable her or embarrass her. Itchy told family members and her teachers, so they could band together to form a *Village of Support*. Lesson learned to expose the *Enemy so that* God can support you through your suffering.

IS IT ME?

Sometimes do you ever think is it me?
Is it me that creates issues for myself?
Is it me that ruffles my feathers?
The pressure in my head builds, till I feel it'll explode.
Ready to point my finger,
But ready to accept what is in me too,
Only unofficially.
Never to fully accept the true problem.
Is it me?
It gotta be
It simply continues to unfold right in front of my eyes.
But wait.
If it's me, how can my eyes see.
Maybe a glimpse of who I could be is the vision at hand.
Unfortunately, that is not me
Desperately wanting...
That glimpse was only a wish.
Never once accomplished.
No patience with an uneasy mind is hard to beat,
Filling complete defeat, because
of this beast born in me.
So back to square one, is it me?

Author: Makayla L. Spencer

CHAPTER TWELVE

Exposing The Enemy – From A Daughter's Point of View

DEALING WITH BIPOLAR Disorder is not recognized by many in the African American community; however, it was no secret in my family. My Grandfather, Father, and I all suffered from this disorder. It is not something that comes and goes like the flu. It sticks with you throughout your everyday life and takes a tremendous toll on your thinking process alongside your physical activities.

It all started for me at the end of the seventh grade going into eighth grade. I was attending Roosevelt Middle School. I was not the popular girl in school, but I had two close friends that made it seem otherwise. We had been friends since the beginning of middle school, but the dynamic of our relationship began to change, and it was not on their behalf. When I look back, I notice a significant change in my temperament and how I handled the situation. I was becoming more impulsive. My mother would have me walk to the library after school, however I wanted to do the same and hang out with other kids. However, instead of hanging out at a park or around the school, I would go to a friend's house. There was one girl who lived on the path I took to the library; so many days, I would go over to her house for hours until I knew my mother was coming to pick me up. I would have to run at least a mile to beat her to the library.

One particular day, I was ten minutes late coming to the library. My mom had called me several times by this time, and I was not answering. As I ran, I saw she was parked outside, so I ran into the library to make it seem like I was there all day, but she knew. I was hot, sweating, out of breath, and smelled like the outside. There was no running away from the trouble I was about to be in. My mom took my phone for the first time. Even though I felt like she had just taken my life away from me, I still felt a sense of ease within myself. It seemed like this impulsive activity was a sort of release for me.

Not long after that incident, my mom and I moved from Detroit to Farmington Hills. It seemed like the other side of the world, with new people and a new environment. The idea of a new start was not so bad, but I knew I would miss the life I had before. However, the enemy was starting to break loose. Around this time is when I began hearing voices. Voices that would put me down or scream thoughts of self-harm, but at the time, I tried to ignore them. While entering the eighth grade, I was in a new school, with no friends or anybody that looked like they wanted a new friend. I started to feel like a loner, which did not help with the voices that would constantly put me down. Over time, I learned how to distinguish the difference whether the voices were realistic or just in my head. I noticed I became a lot more upbeat and willing to branch out during this process. I began making friends, joining sports, and even behaving well in and out of school. My grades were not a 4.0, but I was learning much better in this school district than in the others I attended.

It was close to 2010, and high school was soon approaching. At this time, my friends and I would attend high school football and basketball games, trying to get familiar with the atmosphere before being thrown to the wolves. People made High School seem scary and full of drama, which I later came to find had some truth to the stories I had heard. As I entered the ninth grade, I was still cool with the same people from eighth grade, so I felt like I had a support system. But that dwindled soon after, and many people started to branch off into other cliques.

So now I was back to having just two friends. These two were always there for me, and one even introduced me to my first love. At the time, I had no interest in taking anyone seriously because I knew that it would take more out of me than I could handle. I was already fighting the enemy inside, and I did not need any extra pressure. But as a young girl, I took on the challenge anyway. He and I were like Bonnie and Clyde, in a sense. We grew closer as the days went on; he was two years older, so I felt he was mature enough to handle the things I would throw his way. Not too long after we started dating, I began to open up to him about the voices I had been hearing and how I did not easily control my moods. At this point, I felt like he took that as an advantage for himself. Most people would be nervous or tell me to seek help. But he was interested, which made me love him more. Just because he was older did not mean that he knew everything, as I thought.

Many would say that this was the real turning point in my behavior, but it was not. I noticed that he had an edgy side to himself, which I saw as an excellent characteristic. However, my impulsivity and his edginess were not a good combination. We began to become toxic to each other. We would skip school, skip class while in school, run away late at night, sneak each other into the other's house, and even let each other live in the other house without our parents knowing. It was getting to a point where we would do anything risky to get a release for us both. But things went left after a while, the thrills did not satisfy him anymore, and my bipolar ways were starting to show more and more. He would call me crazy, delusional, and psychotic; this made me sink into a low place. I began accepting what he said and let him continue to mistreat me. Things had gotten very physical at a point in the relationship, which I kept to myself for the longest. As I grew up, I remember the abuse my mother went through. At the time, I did not think the actions were right or wrong. I felt it was just a phase that would soon pass through, but I was wrong. My first cutting experience was due to the enemy slowly defeating me and the pain from the relationship; it was all so confusing. Later after I found myself creating unhealthy friendships and getting into drama that had nothing to do with me, but I felt that I had to prove myself to keep people close.

I made it well into my sophomore year of high school, and there were even more changes than I could handle. While my mother and I were still new to the neighborhood, we found support within our community through our congregation as Jehovah's Witness. Now personally, I was not for this at all. Simply because while growing up, I saw my mom attend both church and the kingdom hall, which I never understood. I felt as though my relationship with God was nonexistent; one reason is that I was young, and secondly, I did not have enough time to grasp the information being taught. However, moving to Farmington seemed to be where I could build a relationship with God because we were more stable and consistent with going to Kingdom Hall. But it seemed as though something was still a little off. The requirements and expectations that we were being held to did not seem realistic as a child; not celebrating holidays, not going to Prom, and not hanging out with "worldly people." I had a hard time connecting to those that were a part of the congregation. Constantly being judged because of my appearance or whom I hung around.

For these to be the people that represent us as a whole, I felt misled. It was manipulative, and it was presented as though God did not want an enjoyable life for humans, and I began to accept that soon after my mother stopped attending and joined New Hope Missionary Baptist Church.

Furthermore, because of these experiences, I adjusted to being unhappy. I was becoming more comfortable with the idea of being crazy. By 2012, the enemy was fully exposed. In the spring of 2012, I began going through manic and depressive episodes. Due to the multiple run-away attempts, my mother contacted the police to help find me. I was at a track meet one particular day, and my mom and six officers came to get me.

This was one of the most embarrassing experiences to date. Once I was detained, I was taken straight to Children's Village, Mandy's Place, under charges of truancy and incorrigibility. This shelter home was for neglected children. When I was there, I had time to think about all I had done. While there I learned to crochet. My Mom and Dad would constantly visit to see if any progress was made, but it took a few months.

Eventually, I was released to my mother and returned to Farmington High School. The agreement for my release was for six-month probation and a tether. As anyone could imagine, nothing was the same as before I left. Once I returned to school, I was now seen as an outcast; people remembered me as the girl who was arrested at the track meet. The word had gotten around that I was taken to juvenile and had mental issues. Many people took advantage of this and bullied me due to my situation.

Within the next week, I was admitted to the Havenwyck Mental Facility. I had another cutting experience and had stopped taking my medication, so my mother sought immediate help. While returning to school, I was no longer on the tether; this tarnished my reputation entirely. I went from the fabulous laid-back freshman to a boy-crazed bipolar misfit.

ALONE

Don't leave me alone through the pain I endure…
Not from the flesh,
From my heart and mind.
Don't leave me alone at night,
It leaves time to question.
The questions of who I truly am.
Don't leave me alone in the cold,
Hold me tight, to let me know you're there
Don't leave me alone when the tears start flowing…
The thoughts are jumbled,
Overwhelmed.
Feels tight and has no air to breathe…
HELP! HELP! I scream…
Nobody hears me.
HELP! HELP! Someone help me.
Don't leave me alone with myself!
… HELP!

Author: Makayla L. Spencer

Once released from Havenwyck, I returned home, but things were more than rocky within the household. My Mother had been stricter than ever and followed my probation rules to the T. I was no longer allowed to stay home by myself or go anywhere alone. I would have to go to my grandmother's while my mom was working, which I was not fond of. This caused a physical fight altercation between my mom and me.

This resulted in the police being called, and they escorted me to my grandmother's. After the incident, my mom had enough, so she placed me back into Children's Village, but this time under maximum security. From August 2012 to October 2012, my dad was the only person to visit, making me feel like my mom did not care or love me anymore. I had gotten overly depressed and gained 70 pounds, totaling 220 pounds. My self-esteem had dropped tremendously, and I no longer saw my self-worth. Being in maximum security gave me time to think on a much higher level. I looked forward to changing something, it did not have to be significant, but I knew it was time to change.

It is now the fall of 2012, and I was being released from Children's Village a second time, I was now under my dad's care, and I soon moved in with his parents because of his job hours. Alongside the release, I was now attending a new school called Fitzgerald High School. Again, I was in a new environment, around too many new faces. For my entire eleventh-grade year, I kept to myself. I did not see the need for associating and letting anyone else in. I knew change was needed and began to think of life-harming changes. In December, I had another suicide attempt by taking 250 tranquilizers while my grandparents were at the Kingdom Hall. They came home and found me passed out on the bathroom floor and immediately called 911. My grandfather performed CPR until the medics arrived. This was one of the scariest times for everyone, even me. I was soon admitted to Children's Hospital and transferred to Kingswood Mental Hospital, where I stayed for three weeks. Because of this, my maternal grandfather went into a manic episode because he had stopped taking his medication due to him praying for me all day. He was admitted into Receiving Hospital shortly after.

THE MONSTER

Depression is a monster,
Not the kind under your bed.
The kind that hangs overhead.
Follows your every step but comes
when most inconvenient.
Feels like I'm drowning,
Drowning in my thoughts.
I feel them flowing wanting to be heard.
Moving to my mouth,
Cutting off my air,
All these thoughts are trying to become words.
The words form the feelings from inside.
Still drowning and fighting.
Trying to swim to the top,
But then the monster is there,
Pulling me back under.
Depression
As I sink, I see the light fade.
The shine and glow I once had.
The bright vibrancy is now dark and gloomy.
The beautiful creation I once saw,
Now see nothing.

No matter how warm the water is,
No matter how bright the sun shines,
No matter how big and bright my smile is,
No matter how warm a hug can be,
No matter what.
Nothing can get this monster off me

Author: Makayla L. Spencer

I kept to myself at school, and nobody even recognized that I had been gone for almost a month. This was even more devastating because I had no one that cared. I soon saw no point in life and contemplated dropping out of high school until one day at a parent-teacher conference. Every teacher said they saw potential in me and did not want to see me leave, but one teacher, in particular, reached out, more concerned than the others. She asked my reasoning behind dropping out, which at the time was very immature and selfish.

She went on to see that my GPA was lower than 1.0; therefore, she offered me a chance to redeem myself. If I could raise my GPA above 2.5 before the trimester was over, I could join the student government committee as a representative. I raised my GPA and going into my Senior I was now a part of the committee. Once I heard that I felt like I had a purpose.

In my senior year my grades improved significantly. I was now holding a 4.0 GPA throughout the remaining trimester. I joined the cheerleading team and became captain and lost over 60 pounds. Life had seemed to turn around for me. Even though I had been in and out of mental hospitals, juvenile centers, and many manic episodes, life was not over for me. The enemy creeps over my shoulder daily, but I refuse to let it conquer me. I may have to take medicine every day and see a therapist, but it helps me understand myself and assures me that I am not alone. I was suffering from bipolar disorder and feeling alone was not good company. It only led me to impulsive and risky behaviors, self-harm, and resenting myself. These three things are well in my past, and I plan to keep them there.

My relationship with God has grown, and my relationship with my family is stronger than ever. It took a village to raise me, and it may take a village to conquer the enemy.

At a certain point in life, I knew that Michigan was not all that was out there for me. While in High School, I had an opportunity to travel to Spain with a Spanish 2 class. This was a great chance to explore life outside Farmington and Detroit, but at the time, my mind was elsewhere. My image was more at risk, plus my sanity was borderline questionable to everyone. So, when TSU came around, I saw nothing but the stars. I had never been to Nashville, making it even more of an out-the-blue decision. However, through many of my experiences in prior school: I saw that I felt more comfortable around my race. So, an HBCU was perfect for me. Life seemed like it would be so much easier, and people would be friendlier. No parents would be close by to interrupt my lifestyle choices, and at most, I would be doing whatever I pleased. Now I can say this was an impulsive decision, but it helped me learn a lot more about myself. Now the feeling before even leaving for college was through the roof.

I believed that I would get my degree in less than four years. I believed that I would join a sorority and a few organizations on campus. Also, I thought I would be a majorette dancing—all these plans when I was just planning to drop out of high school. I knew I needed to make my parents proud and wanted a couple notches under my belt that would speak for me.

Now TSU is in my grasp; I'm alone and feeling lost. I heard that this was a normal feeling. But I was used to being outgoing and just falling into my circle of friends. Luckily, I had a friend back home that I could talk to regularly. I constantly felt as if I would be a nobody on this campus of extraordinary personalities. How could I join anything if I knew no one? As time went on, I started speaking to people in the halls of my dorms and even saw some people from schools back home. All so bittersweet; it was like I left home for a new start, a more consistent start, hoping to come back with a cleaned-up identity. But seeing old faces made me recognize I was still that same girl that moved around and never really blossomed into herself. Noticing that running away was not the answer but running within. Through every experience the beast was present, but I was too.

MASTER & EXPLORE

Since day one I heard
Master your learnings
Branch off and explore
My eyes are open to dreams and experiences
Much bigger much better

Exponential potential to master new learnings
Excited to branch off and explore
Since day one space was needed
Time for my vision and soul to explore

Fear, happiness
Anxiety, readiness
Impulsive, well planned
All geared with the tools needed
To become much bigger much better

While steered off the path with this passenger
I needed time to explore and master me
However, this space to learn became...
Lessons of studying and weighing options

Much more was needed within
Master your feelings
Branch off and open up
Was more of what became in time

Space became too grand
And that soul was at a standstill
No more exploration,
Mastering peace was needed

Since day one
That was never there.
Peace…
So ready for an open soul to explore

Never adjusted to the run
Just space to see and explore who was the soul
See that the master was since day one me!

Author: Makayla L. Spencer

HELPFUL HINTS

- Observe A Persons' Behavior
- Journal Incidents & Mood Swings Weekly
- Learn the Person Triggers
- Suicide Help Line **1-800-273-8255** readily available
- National Domestic Violence Help Line **1-800-799-7233 or text 88788**
- House of Kadence – LaChetta Johnson Founder/ CEO
- http://www.houseofkadence.com
- Teach or Encourage Coping Skills – Ex: write poetry, exercise, draw, music, crochet, sew, dance, sing, etc.
- Share Behavior with Pediatrician/Physician
- Communicate with School Administrators & Teacher
- Meet with Schools Social Worker
- Request paperwork to fill out 504 Plan for Students with Disabilities
- Familiarize yourself and family members with your local Police Officials
- Seek a licensed Therapist/Psychotherapist
- Set up an appointment for Evaluation by a Psychiatrist
- Make sure they are taking the medicine

- ◦ Inquire if injections are an option over pills
- ◦ Inquire about how the meds work with birth control pills
- When placed on medication, watch for side effects
- Talk to the Pharmacist and read over the tips and information
- Become the Voice of your Child
- Most important, explain what is happening to them
- Encourage your child to talk to you freely

GLOSSARY

Abilify – Aripiprazole (Generic Name) for depression

DV – Domestic Violence

Enemy – Bipolar

Good Ole Boy's Club – Racist

Lack Luster – Uninspiring

Lamotrigine - Lamictal (Brand Name) mood stabilizer to delay manic depression episodes also used for epileptic seizures

Reaganomics – Impoverished Economic Status

Sugar Honey Iced Tea – Shit

Buildings that no longer exist in Detroit are italicized.

ANXIETY COPING STATEMENTS

1. I feel good Today
2. I will take one Day at a time
3. I'm in a Safe place
4. I need to Trust the process I'm okay
5. This is a Safe space
6. I can handle the way I feel
7. The fact of the matter is I feel Anxious
8. Thoughts are not Facts
9. I can go Write down/journal my feelings
10. I can take care of Myself

Printed in the United States
by Baker & Taylor Publisher Services